THE TIE-DYED KAFTAN MURDERS

MILLIE RAVENSWORTH

TO THE READER...

This novel features a number of cryptic crossword clues. Don't worry. You don't need to understand the clues to enjoy the story but if you did want a head start on solving this murder mystery, here they are...

- At first she's impressed, but you ultimately fail – she'll have foreseen it all (5)
- Welsh songwriting legend: "I loved opera", occasionally (4)
- Killer puzzle? Nothing grand, even if it is the wrong way round (8)
- Like vermouth, metallic element is a dangerous thing to consume (9)
- Athena regularly has it, but Hecate always partakes (3)

- Hide hides hide of opossum with heads of Indian cobras: it's a serious offence (8)
- Naval officer is on dangerous substance (8)
- Somewhat lacking a tobacconist, returning Greek leaves, or all sorts of plants (9)
- First crime scene: gendarme gets confused without me (6)
- Stress about papers? There's not much you can do about it (8)

1

Izzy King stepped out of the rear door of Cozy Craft to find Penny noisily hauling a round-bottomed kettle barbecue through the gate into the tiny back yard.

"I was just going to say I'm off to the Frambeat Gazette meeting," said Izzy, "and then—" She waved a confused hand at the dusty spherical barbecue, giving her cousin and business partner a look which she hoped was sufficiently bewildered to convey her questions about the appearance of a barbecue in their back yard.

"For Easter," said Penny, as though that answer explained everything (which it did not).

Izzy maintained her look.

"I saw it in the alley," said Penny. "It was sort of by Dougal Thumbskill's, but I don't know if it's his."

The row of Georgian shops along the edge of the marketplace in Framlingham had tiny yards at the rear, and a communal access which was supposed to be kept clear.

"It will be perfect," said Penny.

"For Easter?" said Izzy, just checking.

"Easter," Penny nodded.

Izzy decided questions would have to wait until later. She was running late for the meeting and it was her turn to take biscuits.

Izzy said goodbye to Monty in his box by the counter and stepped out.

It was April, Easter was round the corner, and even though it was definitely not barbecue weather, the sun was high and shining bright, bringing extra vibrancy to the flowers growing in planters at the edge of the marketplace and the hanging baskets outside the Crown Hotel.

Between a gap in the old buildings at the bottom end of the marketplace was a walkthrough to the Co-Op supermarket. Izzy popped in, grabbed a packet of biscuits, and carried on along Riverside and up Fore Street to the Millers Field sheltered accommodation building. Millers Field nestled close to the heart of the town and was the home to many older residents, including Izzy's grandma, as well as the editor-in-chief of the *Frambeat Gazette*, a community-produced local newspaper.

In the centre's day room, Izzy found the rest of the editorial team already waiting for her. They called themselves the editorial team even though they were the newspaper's entire workforce.

"Just when we thought you were never going to appear," said Glenmore Wilson in his usually curmudgeonly manner. He was an elderly, one-armed former military man of Jamaican descent, and Izzy sometimes wondered which of these adjectives contributed most to his somewhat brusque manner.

"I come bearing biscuits," she said, placing the packet by the fresh pot of tea on the table. Tariq opened them with perhaps unseemly speed, but at least remembered to offer one to Glenmore and Annelise before tucking in.

"Do you think it's too early in the year for a barbecue?" said Izzy.

"Yes," said Tariq.

"Depends," said Annelise.

"Is that a genuine question, or an idea for an article in next week's paper?" asked Glenmore.

Izzy shrugged and sat.

Annelise regarded the iced biscuit she now held. "Aren't party rings a children's biscuit?"

"Definitely," said Glenmore, putting four of them along the edge of his saucer. "Now, we are well served for general articles for the next week or so—"

"Actually, I wondered if we had room for an article about Sybil Catchpole?" said Annelise.

"Catchpole, Catchpole," said Glenmore, frowning. "We ran her obituary a few months back."

"No," said Annelise. "We held off because there was the inquest. The funeral is now allowed to go ahead and it would seem timely. I know her daughter, Gwen, and—"

"We could bump the piece about the castle to the following week," suggested Izzy.

"We've got a big article planned about the children's Easter egg hunt for then," said Annelise.

"Then the week after."

"I'm really proud of that castle piece," pouted Tariq.

Glenmore made a throaty grumble. "Framlingham Castle has stood on that hill for more than eight hundred years, Tariq. I suspect the article can be published in a fortnight and still remain relevant."

"By the way, Izzy," said Annelise, "my friend Gwen asked if you do toys."

"Toys?"

"Sewing. Whether you make teddy bears and soft toys and such?"

Izzy thought on it. Cozy Craft certainly had the materials for making toys, including a varied selection of lustrous button eyes, but she wouldn't have normally considered herself a toymaker. "Never say never," she shrugged.

"A terrible motto to live one's life by," said Glenmore. "All the regular features in order?" He peered short-sightedly at his papers and then at Izzy. "Madame Zelda's horoscopes completed for this week?"

"They are," she said.

Another throaty grumble. "And this year, will she be including a list of things that Geminis would like for their birthdays, including the names of shops they can be bought from?"

Izzy felt she maintained her poker face well. "I don't know. I would have to ask her."

Tariq hid a smile. The true identity of Madame Zelda was an open secret in the group, but one they all still played along with.

"And the cryptic crossword?" said Glenmore.

"Yes, about that," said Annelise, smoothing out a piece of paper on the table. "This is the last one. For now at least."

"The last?"

"I get them sent to me in batches. This last one came alone and I've not received any more for, well, months."

"You haven't chased our crossword setter?" said Glenmore.

"I don't have contact details," said Annelise. "Socrates always sends them to the library with no return address."

Izzy had long assumed that 'Socrates' was a pen name for Annelise, just as Izzy carried on the pretence of being Madame Zelda. Maybe Annelise had run out of the time or energy to create more crosswords.

"Then we'd best enjoy this final crossword," said Glenmore.

There was a buzz from Izzy's phone. It was a message from her boyfriend, Marcin.

Maybe you would like to move some of your things in this weekend. I have cleared some drawer space. XX.

The message came as a surprise, although perhaps it shouldn't have been much of one. Only last week Madame Zelda had suggested to Aquarius readers that they should bite the bullet and invite that special someone to be a closer part of their lives. Madame Zelda didn't mention this was because certain Geminis were tired of sharing a bedroom with their dad's mobile disco equipment. That might have been too specific.

Izzy returned to the shop later to find Penny still in the back yard. She had covered the barbecue drum in cling film and was now slathering it with a thick layer of papier-mâché. Monty the corgi was sniffing at the paper gloop with interest.

Izzy frowned for a minute and then clicked her fingers in understanding. "For Easter!"

"That's what I *said*," said Penny.

2

When the layer of papier-mâché had dried, Penny Slipper peeled the oval shape off the top of the drum. The cling film layer made it relatively easy and there was something inordinately satisfying about the act of pulling it away: a neat sense of victory, like stripping poorly stuck wallpaper, or taking the protective plastic off a phone for the first time, or tossing a pancake and having it land perfectly in the pan.

Penny had been working in Framlingham for a little over a year and living in the comfy little flat above the shop. Just because she was taking pleasure from papier-mâché success, didn't mean that life here was dull or lacking entertainments, but she had certainly learned to enjoy the benefits of living in a small community far from the loveless and sometimes alienating life she'd had in London.

Izzy came out into the yard and inspected the domed creation.

"Either I make a second one to complete a whole egg," said Penny, "or we bury it in pretend straw to hide the missing half."

"And you're going to cover it in one of those new spring fabrics?" said Izzy.

Penny nodded. "A big, delicious looking Easter egg. Except it's not a real chocolate egg, which is a shame. Imagine."

"I saw some new cakes in the bakery. A chocolate brownie with a mini egg on the top. We could get some of those."

Penny frowned. "They've always sold brownies."

"But these have mini eggs on top. We need to keep up with the times, Penny."

There was a creak at the gate and a face looked over, a pair of small accusing eyes set into a tired, wrinkled face. "Ah ha! *My* barbecue!"

"Is it yours, Dougal?" said Penny. "Sorry, I didn't— I'll get it cleaned up for you!"

The eyes frowned, disapproving rather than angry, before he sank behind the gate again.

"I'll clean it good as new, Mr Thumbskill!" Penny shouted after him.

"I'll get him an Easter egg brownie too," said Izzy.

PENNY SPENT the afternoon updating the window dressing for the Cozy Craft sewing shop. New deliveries of beautiful spring fabrics set the theme, so the colours were fresh greens, pinks and yellows. Penny's huge papier-mâché Easter egg was covered in one of the new fabrics, then she tied a broad pink ribbon around its middle. It took centre stage, in front of the beautiful old treadle sewing machine that was often a feature in the window.

Penny went outside to check on the display and was pleased by the effect. It was very eye-catching, although Penny did wonder what they would do with the giant Easter egg once they changed the display.

"Easter egg piñata," Izzy suggested when Penny went back inside. "Fill it with sweets."

Penny wrinkled her nose. "Is a piñata appropriate for Easter?"

"Actually, in the Middle Ages, piñata – from the Italian for 'fragile pot' – were part of the Lent celebrations before Easter."

"That sounds like it came straight from one of your *Frambeat Gazette* 'Word Nerd' columns."

"Maybe," said Izzy.

Penny had some shop accounts to look at. Izzy put on the kettle for a cup of tea, then brought out two mini-egg brownies she'd bought from Wallerton's bakery.

"So," said Izzy with heavy emphasis, "Marcin said I could take some things round to his place when I go over this Saturday."

"Uh huh. Next step in the relationship."

"Right. But what does he mean by *things*? A toothbrush? All of my clothes? My one-man-band apparatus?"

"I wasn't there, Izzy. You probably need to clarify with Marcin. Unless he left it deliberately open, to see what you make of it."

A smile spread across Izzy's face. "Oh yeah, that could be it! In other words, I can do what I want?"

"That's not exactly what I—"

"—I'll tell you what, he has the most enormous dining table, it will be perfect for dressmaking and crafts. We're always fighting each other for table space at home. Dad wants it for tinkering with his amps and speakers, and Mum always has tons of paperwork for her job. I've never seen anything at all on Marcin's table; it's completely wasted."

"Unless," said Penny, wary of the way Izzy had already mentally staked her claim. "Unless he *likes* it empty. Some people are like that."

Izzy gave her a look. It was the look you'd expect from a child who'd just been told Santa wasn't real. Penny opened up the laptop and sought refuge in the accounts.

"Watch this, Izzy," she said, picking the mini egg off the top of her brownie. "With magic I have recreated the old brownie. Oh but look – now it's a new brownie!" She put the mini egg back.

Izzy rolled her eyes. "Don't pretend you didn't want one. I can take it from you if you don't want it."

Penny pulled her plate protectively away from Izzy.

The door opened and a woman walked in.

Penny placed her brownie back on the plate and gave the woman a moment to gaze around the shop. Penny and Izzy had tried their best to make the place friendly and welcoming. The floorboards and shelving were in an old, polished wood which had its own warm glow and created a pleasing contrast with the fabrics displayed on shelves and in upright bolts. Ribbons, trims and other haberdashery were mostly at the rear of the shop, but some baskets were placed strategically, so that people could absorb the possibilities as they browsed.

"Can I help you?" Penny asked.

"Lovely place you have here," said the woman. She was well-spoken, had bright pink skin, and the look of a woman who was not yet middle-aged but was taking a good run up at it. She stepped forward with a hand extended. "Gwen Codling. My friend said I should come in."

Izzy tried to respond but still had brownie in her mouth. She swallowed quickly. "Annelise?"

"Yes," said Gwen. "I go to her library book group. I wanted to ask whether you do commission work?"

"We do undertake commissions, but we always provide a quote," said Penny. "It can be expensive." When providing sewing services it was a constant battle against the expectations set by fast fashion.

"*Pfft*," said Gwen with a lightly dismissive wave of her hand. "The cost is not the issue here." She gave a rueful smile. "I sound like I have money to burn, and I definitely do not. What I mean to say is that cost is less important than getting the job done well."

"Annelise mentioned it might have something to do with toys?" Izzy prompted.

"Yes," said Gwen. "My mother, Sybil, died a few months ago, and I'm interested in getting some memory bears made. Are you familiar with memory bears?"

"A sort of keepsake of a departed person?" said Izzy.

"So, this would be a teddy bear or something similar,

made using fabrics from your mother's wardrobe?" asked Penny.

"Exactly," said Gwen. "It's possible we might use some of her cushions, home furnishings. That sort of thing as well."

Izzy leaned in. "How many do you need?"

Gwen gave a sad smile. "Donny, Josie and Mary; all mine. My brother doesn't have any. They will miss her dearly. I'd like one too, so we're looking at four in total. They don't have to be bears, either. I'm very much open to suggestions."

"Are the children very young?" asked Izzy. "There are safety considerations if they're tiny."

"No. All secondary school age. And I picture the bears as being more ornamental than anything."

"More freedom for us then," said Izzy.

Penny could see the gleam in Izzy's eye and knew she was already mentally embarking on this new project.

"Not sure if it helps," said Gwen, "but I need to pop over to mum's place this evening. So if you were available to come along and take a look, you could see her things. Her style is worth seeing in the flesh, I think. It should influence what you do."

Izzy beamed at the prospect, and Penny could relate to her enthusiasm. "It could help. If we're to come up with a good solution, then understanding your mother's style and personality is important. Her place is local, yes?"

"Avalon Cottage, just out of town on Brook Lane. Say, six o'clock?"

"Ideal," said Penny.

"Oh, and while I'm here, I wonder if you'd mind popping

a poster in your window for a charity event?" Gwen asked. "Lovely display by the way."

She handed Penny a poster. Penny looked at the bright colours, the images that had a cute, potato-print simplicity about them.

"An Easter egg hunt? Of course we will," said Penny. "Brick Lane copse."

"I do like an Easter egg hunt," said Izzy.

"It looks as though it's meant for children, Izzy," said Penny with a laugh.

"You should come!" said Gwen. "Easter Sunday. There is no age limit. Chocolate indulgence for everyone, and we'll be raising funds to put more bat boxes up in the trees. It's a beautiful local wood."

"We will definitely put the poster up; and it sounds as if we might join you on the day," said Penny.

"Oh yes. You had us at chocolate," said Izzy.

The woman left with a cheery wave.

"Now, remind me what you're giving up for Lent," Penny said to Izzy.

"Starting one mad creative project without finishing the last one?"

"Right. These memory bears definitely sound like a mad creative project."

"It's a commission."

Penny shrugged. "Just reminding you. Helping you keep your Lent vows."

"And what are you giving up?" said Izzy.

"I'm giving up on denying myself things that make me happy," said Penny and put the brownie in her mouth.

3

"Have you ever made a memory bear before?" Penny asked Izzy as they walked along narrow streets bounded by neat pink houses and greenery to Gwen's mum's cottage on Brook Lane.

"I have made one," said Izzy, "but it wasn't called that."

"Oh?"

"Yeah, mum used to have a corduroy dress that she really liked. When it wore out I made a draught excluder with a cat's head for her."

"Hm. Similar idea," said Penny, although she wasn't sure that it really was. Gwen had said she was open to ideas, but deploying her dead mother's fabrics as an energy saving device seemed slightly disrespectful.

Brook Lane was only a ten-minute walk, but Avalon Cottage itself was down the end of a longer track. Apart from a larger house built a short distance to the side behind some trees, it was a truly isolated location.

Izzy absorbed the exterior as they approached. "This place is very cute. Small, but proper flint walls."

They rang the bell and waited outside.

"Flint's interesting, isn't it?" said Penny. "Flint knives are a thing, hard to imagine them being made from the same stuff as this."

Izzy ran a finger around one of the stones set into the wall. It had a dull sheen. "A lot of pebbles you dig up in the garden round here look like this on the inside, if you smash them open with a hammer. Ask me how I know."

Penny rolled her eyes.

"It's called knapping. Our prehistoric ancestors did skilful knapping to make their axe heads and whatnot, but it's bashing just the same. You break off sharp flakes and make a blade."

"You've tried it, haven't you?" said Penny, incredulous.

"What? You make it sound weird. To be honest the weird thing for me is that some people *haven't* tried it."

Gwen opened the door and smiled. "You found it."

"It's a lovely house," said Penny. "Izzy and I were just admiring the exterior."

"Traditional but quirky. That's the way my mother was," said Gwen, and closed her eyes for a moment. "Both of my parents, I guess."

Izzy could see the traditional but quirky aspect inside of the cottage. "I've heard this style described as maximalist. I very much approve."

Penny turned to Izzy. "Is that like the opposite of being minimalist?"

"It is," said Izzy. "It's for people who want to embrace all of the colours and crazy eclectic collectables."

Gwen gave a small laugh. "That describes my mother to a tee. If she had lived a thousand lifetimes she could never have involved herself with all of the things she wanted to. Every time I saw her she'd have found a new rabbit hole to explore."

Izzy found it delightful. There were display cabinets and shelving units with collections that ranged from mid-century pottery to antique flower presses. The walls featured clusters of brightly coloured artwork and many potted plants.

"A lot of these are hers," said Gwen. "The art, I mean. An amazing artist. Obviously, the plants were hers too." She smiled tiredly. "It takes me over an hour to water all of them. I've been doing it for months. My mother never met a house plant she didn't like."

The plants were suspended from the ceiling in macrame hangers, and also arranged in cascades from an old step ladder and other plant stands.

"Has it been a while since she died then?" Penny asked.

"It has, although we've not yet been able to lay her to rest. There was an autopsy because of the unusual circumstances."

Penny and Izzy both paused, curious for Gwen to expand on her statement, but mindful of being crass or insensitive.

"I probably didn't mention," said Gwen, with a small shake of her head "she was poisoned—" She cleared her throat and started afresh. "Poisoned herself. An accident."

Penny's hand went to her mouth. "How awful. I am so very sorry."

Gwen nodded. "Her garden was an important part of her life. You never stop to think that the plants out there can be dangerous. I'll show you outside once we are done in here."

Izzy took the cue to examine some of the textiles, so she picked up a cushion. "I think she liked William Morris prints, so we could incorporate some of these."

"Take a look upstairs, she had all sorts. Wait until you see the bedroom lined with sari silk, and the mannequin in the bathroom."

Izzy didn't need asking twice, she trotted up the stairs, closely followed by Penny.

"Take your time," called Gwen. "I'll put the kettle on."

They went into the bedroom.

"Oh my," said Penny.

The bed was a modern version of a four poster, with a tubular metal frame. Silk hung from the top rail in a riotous display of jewelled colour. The window had a similar treatment, and there were hangings around the walls too.

"I bet it's like stained glass when the sun shines through," said Izzy.

"Some people's houses are like time capsules, aren't they?" said Penny. "But this place seems to have collected something from every decade since..."

"...The seventies," Izzy finished the thought. "Definitely getting a seventies counter-culture vibe."

"A hippie?"

Izzy shrugged and moved over to a dressing table. There were three hat stands, each holding a velvet hat. One was shocking pink, one was a vibrant green, and the third orange.

On the wall behind was an antique fan made from blue ostrich feathers.

Penny went to the window and gently stroked the drapes. "She was someone who loved colour. There is so much to work with here. We can make each bear a gorgeous mixture of colour, yet they will all be completely different."

"Agreed," said Izzy. She opened the huge wooden wardrobe and flicked through hangers. Penny came to join her. "I'm going to take some pictures. We can review them back at the shop."

"I had no idea there was going to be so much to take in," said Izzy.

"These are all fairly modern," said Izzy, holding up a sleeve. "And still so colourful. I love the fact that she owned a rainbow hoodie!"

Penny smiled. "I know what you mean. We have some funny expectations about what older people wear."

"Let's check out the bathroom."

It was oddly spacious for a small cottage. Izzy guessed that at some point in the past a bedroom had been sacrificed to add indoor plumbing. There was room for all of the usual fitments, and also a mannequin in the corner, adorned with a long evening dress in pale lilac.

"I have never seen anything like this," said Penny.

Izzy wasn't sure whether she meant the dress, or a bathroom which seemed to have a resident woman standing in the corner, overseeing everything.

They both drifted over to look at the dress. It oozed seventies chic with its simple bold lines and the chunky wooden neck piece.

"How would you wash this? It's part of the dress," said Penny.

"I think you'd have to remove it, then sew it back on after washing," said Izzy.

They went back downstairs. Gwen was in the kitchen. One portion of wall between the cupboard unit and the sink was entirely dominated by shelves for herbs and spices. There were glass jars, smaller at the top, with much larger ones and several tea caddies at the bottom. They were, however, all empty.

Gwen saw them looking. "They had to go for tests. It's bog-standard tea bag tea for us," she said and slightly raised the tea tray she was holding. There was a photo album on one end of it.

"I thought I might carry this outside and look at the photos while we inspect the garden," she said.

The back garden was beautifully maintained, with deep borders that would be a riot of colour in the summer. A large tree stood at the far end. The table was positioned in a sunny corner that was sheltered from any wind.

Izzy opened one of the albums, nudging it over so Penny could see it too.

"It was a great idea to see the house," said Penny. "She must have been a fascinating person."

"She was, er, complex, I guess."

Izzy and Penny flicked through the album. They found a young woman with striking features and naturally curly hair staring back at them. Their guess that she'd been a bit of a hippie appeared to be fairly close to the mark.

"Ooh, proper Cleopatra eyeliner, I love it!" said Izzy,

pointing at a picture where Sybil was wearing the dress from the bathroom.

"She enjoyed a touch of drama, that's for sure," said Gwen with a smile. "She caused a bit of a sensation in the seventies with a book of hers."

"Book?" said Penny.

"*The Golden Bell.* It was quite the craze. Full of puzzles, with a promise of buried treasure as a prize."

Izzy had never heard of it, but made a mental note to track down a copy.

"Can I take some pictures with my phone?" asked Penny, indicating the album. "We thought it might make it easier for us to work through our thoughts when we're back in the shop."

"Of course, go ahead."

While Penny captured some pictures, Izzy gazed around at the garden. Magnolias and winter jasmine stood above and behind a herb garden of lavender and rosemary. Spring had not yet properly sprung, but Izzy could imagine the place full of colour and buzzing bees in a few weeks' time. The tree at the bottom had smooth bark. There was a brass plaque, faded with grime, screwed to the tree. Susan Catchpole, 1927 – 1977.

"My grandma," Gwen called down to her. "Dad's mum."

A movement from the middle distance drew Izzy's attention. Someone was waving from the other side of a rustic trellis fence.

"Gwen, someone is trying to get your attention," she said.

4

wen looked over. "Oh. Alison! Horace! Join us, will you? There's fresh tea in the pot."

To Izzy's amusement, the trellis section was lifted and swung open. "A fence that is actually a gate." Beyond the trellis was another garden and, further off, the neighbouring house Izzy had seen on the way in.

Two older people stepped through. Both were slim, bright-eyed, and their lined skin tanned by something other than the British sunshine. Maybe it was the man's check shirt and the woman's denim dress, but to Izzy, they looked like two sinewy Old West pioneers: invigorated rather than run down by a life of hard labour.

"Alison and Horace are my godparents," said Gwen. "They spent a lot of time with Sybil."

"Oh, we have known Sybil and Ivor more years than we care to remember," said the man. "Horace Atkinson." His handshake was strong and unrestrained.

"You're friends of Gwen?" asked the woman, Alison.

Gwen introduced everyone and, as everyone settled at the outdoor table for tea, explained her ideas for the memory bears.

"Well that sounds like a great idea," said Alison. "I, for one, would very much like to see Sybil's spirit kept alive in bear form. She was the captain of our little group. She liked to force us out of our comfort zone. She did it for years."

"Oh yes?" Penny asked.

"Let me show you," Alison said, taking the photo album. She flicked through. "Ah! I think it's in this one. Morocco! Horace and I would never have been brave enough to go, but Sybil more or less dragged us over there. We loved it of course."

"That was a wonderful time," said Horace.

Izzy and Penny looked at the picture. The colours had faded somewhat over time, but it only added to the dusty feel of the setting. There was a rough-built wall of stone and, in front of it, four people wearing long, loose kaftans with tie-dyed patterns. One of the men posed with a monkey, and the other held a large snake. Everyone's hair was long, but Horace and Alison were nonetheless very recognisable. Time had indeed weathered but not diminished them.

"What a great picture," said Penny to Alison and Horace. "The other man ... your dad, Gwen?"

"Yes. Ivor. He passed away a few years ago," said Gwen.

"Ivor was less keen on Morocco," said Horace. "Mint tea everywhere when all he ever wanted was a drop of the hard stuff. Even then."

"Horace!" said Alison. "That's enough."

"My dad was an alcoholic," Gwen said plainly. "It's not a secret. Although it's not the first thing I would normally choose to share about him." She gave Horace an admonishing look.

Penny left a dignified pause before leaping in with a smile. "This garden is truly delightful. A real passion of your mum's?"

Izzy was in awe of the way Penny batted away the awkwardness of the moment. Izzy tended to smash through a tense situation like a runaway train. This was why they made a great team.

"She loved to be out here pottering," said Gwen with a smile.

"She knew all the Latin names of plants and everything," said Alison. "Very clever."

"I know Latin," said Horace. "Does that make me clever?"

"That is *solicitor Latin,* Horace. Not at all the same thing. It's dry and dull – not like the names of living things."

Horace held up his hands. Whether he was apologising for the dullness of his profession or just trying to get his wife to back off, Izzy wasn't sure. They had the easy manner of people who had known each other their entire lives. Even their squabbles had had the edges rounded off by time.

Penny glanced at Izzy and stood from the table. "We should probably be getting on now."

Izzy nodded and followed her lead.

"I'll tell you something, though," declared Alison. "Sybil knew better than to eat foxglove any day of the week."

"I'm sorry?" said Penny.

"I can't wrap my head around the idea that she got muddled," said Alison. "A normal person, maybe. Not Sybil."

Gwen sighed, and there was an emotional weight in that sigh. "The inquest is done. It's over. The funeral is arranged and we shall put her to rest."

"Celebrate her life and remember the good times," said Alison.

"I don't know why she wanted it in St Michael's Church," said Horace. "She wasn't a Christian."

"It's the heart of the town, and she was always a friend to the church," Alison put in.

"I still say she'd want something with a bit more oomph. Some spiritual freedom and self-expression."

"I think the church is keen on spiritual freedom and self-expression," said Izzy, recognising a mildly defensive tone in her own voice.

"Some gaiety and colour, I say!" said Horace, tapping the photo in the still open book.

Alison smirked, then laughed.

"Oh, dear. I seem to set the wife off again," he said, both amused and bemused.

"It would be fun..." said Alison.

Gwen seemed to catch whatever it was Alison was thinking and her eyebrows rose in delight. "Those kaftans..."

"They're great for wearing in hot weather," said Alison, "not necessarily the British Spring. And I think the style was very much of the time."

"But you loved them. Mum loved them." Gwen swivelled to Penny and Izzy. "What do you think?"

"What do we think about what?" Penny's brow knitted with confusion.

"Making us some tie-dye kaftans so that we can re-create that picture?" Gwen said.

Izzy looked at the picture again. Four young people laughed in the sunshine. She could see why the idea of re-creating this fun picture appealed.

"There's a monkey and a snake," she pointed out.

"We don't need every single detail to be there," laughed Gwen. "Just the people, having a great time."

"Four tie-dye kaftans?" Penny asked. "At a funeral?"

"Oh, I like that," said Horace.

"We'll take a look at that and get you another quote," said Penny.

"A great big send off," the old man nodded firmly. "Then you and your brother can sell this place and move on with your lives."

"We're not decided on that yet," said Gwen.

Izzy and Penny left the cottage a few minutes later. They walked in silence until they were a way up the road.

"What did you make of all that?" asked Penny.

"We could make four actual life-sized bears and there would still be a ton of fabric left over," said Izzy, forming enormous bear shapes with her arms by way of demonstration. "Kaftans should be easy too."

"Not just the project, I mean what did you make of the people and the situation?"

Izzy nodded. "Hmmm. Where to start? Have I got it right? She accidentally poisoned herself with foxglove?"

"That was my interpretation."

"Despite being a plant expert. And then you have the couple next door with their own weird entrance to the garden. And then that thing about a book Sybil wrote. Very, very interesting."

"It must be tough for Gwen, having to pack away the entirety of a parent's life. An unusual mother. An alcoholic father. The baggage created along the way."

"Perhaps she will find solace in the nice cottage she's probably going to inherit?"

"Wash your mouth out, Izzy King! You're surely not thinking she had some part in her mother's death?"

Izzy shook her head. "No, not at all. Well, not until you mentioned it just now."

5

The following day, Penny set about making an album of all the photos they'd taken of fabrics at Avalon Cottage. Izzy was meant to be finding patterns for making toys but had got distracted by reading the latest edition of the *Frambeat Gazette*.

"Surely you read it when you're putting it together," said Penny.

"I'm trying to do the crossword," said Izzy.

"Succeeding?"

"I've got like two of the clues but most of them make no sense. Get this. Eight down, *First crime scene: gendarme gets confused without me. Six letters.*"

Penny shrugged. "Clouseau?"

"Huh?"

"Inspector Clouseau was a confused French policeman."

"It's not six letters."

Penny looked at her. "You're meant to be doing the teddy

bears. I thought your vows for Lent were to not start one thing without finishing another."

"The crossword isn't a project," sniffed Izzy.

The door to the shop opened. Monty gave a yip of greeting. It seemed to be an automatic reflex at times.

Dougal Thumbskill from the shop next door stepped in. "You done with it then?" he said without greeting.

Penny blinked, then remembered. "Sorry. Yes, Dougal. I've cleaned up your barbecue. Shall I bring it round now?"

"It would be a fine idea," he said. He saw Izzy with the crossword. "It's a good one, isn't it?"

"I don't understand it at all," Izzy admitted. "But it might be the last one we ever have, so I thought I'd give it a go."

"Oh, it's not really that challenging," he said. "A five-minute brainteaser."

"Really? Then what's this one about crime scenes and confused gendarmes."

He frowned. Untrimmed eyebrows came together like two caterpillars kissing. "You want me to tell you?"

"Help me understand how it works."

He grunted and looked at the crossword. "Garden."

"Garden?"

"Garden."

"How?"

He made a noise, a sort of sigh, a sort of hum. A noise that was entirely condescending, as though she was a moron. "The actual answer will be in there somewhere. The first crime scene. Well, that's the garden of Eden where Adam and Eve took the apple, yes? So, the answer is garden."

"And the confused gendarme?"

"Confused is telling us to move things round a bit."

"It's an anagram?"

"Yes, but the clue says 'without me' so we have to remove the 'm' and the 'e' from gendarme. Then unscramble it and you get garden."

"Blimey," said Izzy.

Penny was impressed. She barely understood, but it was impressive.

"Our crossword setter clearly continues the vegetation theme with seven down," he said.

"*Somewhat lacking a tobacconist, returning Greek leaves, or all sorts of plants.* Nine letters." She stared. "Nope."

"It's just words to me," said Penny.

"This one's a bit fiddly," Dougal admitted. "'Somewhat' indicates a section of what follows is needed. 'Returning' indicates that section should be read backwards."

"Er, okay."

"Starting with the 'b' in 'tobacconist' and moving back through the clue, we get 'botagnikcal'."

"Botanical?"

"Right, which isn't quite what we want, but then 'Greek leaves'. Greek is traditionally abbreviated to Gk, and removing these two letters gives 'botanical', which is indeed 'all sorts of plants'."

"That's insanely hard," said Izzy.

"The surface meaning is also intended to refer to someone being dissatisfied with the Greek leaves they've tried in lieu of tobacco," said Dougal. "Very satisfying."

Penny shook her head, amazed. "You like books and puzzles, don't you, Dougal?"

"You know I do."

"Heard of a book called the – what was it? – *The Golden Bell*."

His manner changed immediately. He stiffened and his eyes narrowed suspiciously. "What of it?"

"I wondered if you knew anything about it. We were at the cottage of this woman, Sybil."

"Sybil Catchpole," said Dougal. "Really?"

"Her daughter said she wrote a book."

"You don't know it?" he said, nearly scoffing in derision.

"We do not," said Penny politely.

"Nineteen seventy-eight. It was large hardback book, like a child's picture book but full of painted scenes. She worked in oils I believe. Many of the pictures were clearly based on places round here. There was a story of sorts but—" his eyes gave a rare sparkle of excitement "—here's the thing. Catchpole had buried a treasure, a real eighteen carat bell, somewhere in England and the book provides all the clues to its location."

"Wow," said Izzy. "And where was it?"

"What?"

"The treasure. The golden bell."

He pulled back, smiling. "Never been found. No one has yet solved it."

"What? Forty plus years after publication?" said Penny.

"Indeed."

Penny thought on it. "And an eighteen-carat gold bell is worth...?"

"Tens of thousands, easily," said Dougal. "More, even. Some of us still keep the faith. A number of us still look.

There are members of the Suffolk Searchers Metal Detecting Club who consider it their holy grail. Relying on crude technology rather than brain power to locate it."

"So, you have a copy of this book?" said Penny. "Could we take a look?"

"Certainly not!" he snapped. "I have my notes and charts tucked throughout it. I'm not letting you look at those."

"We don't want to find the treasure."

"That's what they all say." He sniffed firmly. "I will go round and open my rear gate and expect the barbecue promptly." With that, he left, followed by a friendly bark from Monty.

Penny and Izzy looked at each other.

"Sybil buried a fabulous treasure and left a book of clues," said Izzy. "This woman just gets more and more interesting. Makes me wish we'd met her in life."

Penny could only nod in agreement.

6

During their morning coffee break, Izzy pored over her phone, trying to ignore Penny's running commentary about the shop's accounts.

"I made a pie chart to show which of our activities are the most profitable," said Penny. "Take a look."

"Mmmm, pie," said Izzy, without looking up.

"Izzy! Pay attention, will you? We can make good use of this information. Running more workshops is what we need to do, see?"

Izzy looked at the chart which had a large purple section. "Oh, that is good to know. Great work, Penny."

Penny narrowed her eyes. "You're doing that thing where you say what you think I want to hear so that I will shut up and go away."

"Um." Izzy had no answer for that, she knew she'd been rumbled. She gave Penny a small guilty smile.

"What are you looking at anyway? Something has you all distracted."

Izzy turned her phone to show Penny. "Someone has a whole load of sheep's fleeces for sale, and they are so cheap they're almost giving them away."

Penny looked at the picture, zooming in to examine the detail. "Are these straight off the sheep? Surely they need a load of processing to make them into anything? They look a bit grubby if I'm honest. Not planning on turning our whole shop into a wool mill, are you?"

"They do need a lot of processing, which is why this would be properly fun. Just imagine it, Penny! I looked it all up and people do it on a small scale all the time. How brilliant would it be to take wool all the way from sheep to sweater?"

"Izzy, I'm sure I don't need to remind you that you gave up crazy projects for Lent," said Penny.

"Yes, but it won't always be Lent," said Izzy with a waggle of her eyebrows. "And if these are still available when Easter gets here then I will be free to indulge myself."

"One small thing though, isn't the planning of future crazy projects kind of doing the very beginning part of crazy projects? Aren't you indulging the very thing you're not supposed to be doing?" asked Penny.

"You sound just like Marcin," scowled Izzy. "He said the same thing. Surely I can look at things and think about things?"

Penny threw her hands up in the air. "I'm not going to tell you how to live your life Izzy, but if you want your Lent to be about resisting temptation, you need to watch out for it popping up in other places. Now, come, take a look at these photos I've transferred to the laptop."

Penny and Izzy clicked through the pictures from Sybil's house.

"I think I can safely say that this memory bear project will not be about the bears," said Izzy after a few minutes.

"Explain," said Penny.

"It's going to be all about colour."

"Right..." Penny wondered where Izzy was going with this.

"As an example of what I mean, it would be totally wrong for us to make a bear out of a single curtain. Don't get me wrong, she had some nice curtains. It would probably look gorgeous – but it would be wrong. It would not honour Sybil's memory."

"Oh! Yes of course. So we have the job of combining her things in new and exciting ways?" Penny thrilled at the idea. Izzy was absolutely right.

"Exactly. So if we print off all of these pictures, we could cut them up and see what works."

Penny rolled her eyes. "Or we could remember that we live in the twenty-first century and use the computer."

Izzy pulled a face. "Maybe."

Penny knew that Izzy worked better with things that she could touch and feel, so she pondered on a compromise. "Here's what we do. I will screen-grab some small snippets of fabrics from the pictures and arrange them in some sort of palette. We can't rely on the pictures looking true to colour, but it should give us some ideas."

"Good idea," said Izzy. "There's something else we need to discuss with Gwen, too."

Penny had already started creating the palette by picking up neat circles of each colour from a photo and dropping them into a new document in tidy lines. "Uh huh?"

"I wonder if Gwen seriously pictures us taking our fabric shears to everything in the house? That dress on the bathroom mannequin for example: it's a vintage collector's piece. We will do what she says, but I would feel very bad if we chopped it into bits."

"Hm." Penny nodded. "I see what you mean. Let's talk to Gwen."

"One last thing," said Izzy. She pulled out her phone and set a timer. "I'm timing your work."

"My what?"

"You're working on a commission and we haven't even made a quote yet. I'm logging your hours."

Penny was affronted. In the past she had been the one to introduce timers, as Izzy wasn't always focused on the business side of things. Penny had insisted that they needed to charge a realistic price for their time. Now she was being accused of breaking her own rules. "I was just organising our thoughts a little bit." It sounded lame even to her own ears.

"You're making a cute palette because it appeals to your neat and tidy nature, and also because it's fun," said Izzy with a knowing waggle of her eyebrows.

Penny huffed. "Yeah, guilty as charged. I can't believe I've been caught out like that."

"You're only human, I suppose. Come on, let's work on a quote and get back to Gwen."

"You know what though, when we do bespoke work like this we should always challenge ourselves to see whether it might be something we can repeat. I wonder how many people know about memory bears?"

Izzy pulled a face that said she wasn't sure. "If I had to guess, I would say that lots of people have heard of the idea, but not many of them would bring it to mind when they lose a loved one."

"Hm. I wonder if there is a way to address that?" Penny felt as if the very idea was tasteless; but maybe that was just general British squeamishness when it came to talking about death.

"Leaflets in funeral directors, that sort of thing?" Izzy asked.

"Maybe."

GWEN ARRIVED A LITTLE LATER.

"Morning, Gwen. Cup of tea?"

Once they were all settled with a drink and some bourbon biscuits from the kitchenette cupboard, Penny pulled her laptop across the counter. "I've got a quote for you, but it's worth taking a moment to describe the approach we thought we might take. We were bowled over by the colours and fabrics in your mum's house, so we decided to combine them into four very special memory bears. See here, we have started to organise a palette of colours, just to give you an idea." Penny glanced over at Izzy, acknowledging a small sample was all they needed at this point. "Each bear will be made from a palette. The names we've provisionally given to them are here."

Penny pushed the paper document towards Gwen so she could read them.

"Peacock Bear, Autumn Leaf Bear, Houseplant Jungle Bear and Moroccan Souk Bear," read Gwen. "It's like an alternative Spice Girl reunion. They sound delightful, and I can picture how each one might look too." She turned over the page, taking in the rest of the quote and the final figure. "It's all great. This is going to work well, please do go ahead."

"Nice, looking forward to it!" said Izzy. "Can we just check on something, though?"

"Of course," said Gwen.

"Some of the clothes, and maybe some of the textiles, have some value. You don't want us to cut those up, do you?"

Gwen gave a loose shrug and held her hands up. "Ladies, I am in your hands. If you tell me there are things that need to be dealt with in a different way then, please let me know. You can imagine the mammoth task I face in emptying that house. I'd originally imagined it would all go to the charity shop."

Penny leaned in thoughtfully. "I think we can help with that. We'll take the items we need for the bears and point out anything which perhaps ought to be evaluated separately."

"Can I suggest," said Izzy, giving Penny a peculiarly guilty look, "that you take some of the items to the Dress Agency in Wickham Market."

Penny immediately understood the reason for the guilty look. The Dress Agency was the nearest thing – geographically at least – that Cozy Craft had to a competitor.

However, whereas Cozy Craft was a sewing shop that had branched out into commissioned pieces, the Dress Agency had started out as a high-class women's clothing shop which also did alterations and designs. They were, in truth, very different shops, even though they both served the same passions. However, Carmella Mountjoy, owner of the Dress Agency, took a different view: regarding Penny and Izzy as low-class competitors who would steal her business and customers at every opportunity. Two shops that should have been supportive of one another were on very unfriendly terms.

"The Dress Agency," Gwen nodded. "Good, thank you. But if there happens to be anything useful for your own purposes, do help yourselves." Gwen gave a smile. "It all needs to go. Oh—!" She delved into her handbag and presented them with a set of keys for the cottage. "Come and go as you please and, seriously, take any fabrics you wish."

Penny noticed Izzy's muted expression of glee. She might have to work hard to stop Izzy's magpie instinct from grabbing everything.

When Gwen had gone, Penny looked at Izzy. "Carmella Mountjoy? Really?"

Izzy shrugged indifferently. "The woman excels at selling vintage and fashion garments to the frivolous and wealthy. She could help Gwen get a good price. By the way, look at this." On the laptop she clicked to the internet, and an article from a local news site. Penny leaned in and read.

·   ·   ·

A SUFFOLK WOMAN who drank tea containing dried foxglove died through "misadventure" a coroner has ruled. Sybil Catchpole (73) from Framlingham died on 4th December after consuming a herbal tea of her own making which included a number of seeds from the deadly plant. The purple foxglove flower is grown in many UK gardens but all parts of the plant contain the poison cardiac glycoside. This poison is used to make the heart drug, digoxin, but can, if consumed in their natural state, lead to heart attack and death.

Detective Inspector Diddiford of Suffolk Police said that Ms Catchpole had many dried plants and herbs stored in her kitchen and had apparently added the deadly plant to her tea blend before consuming it. Recording the death as misadventure, assistant coroner, Angela Blatch, said, "Despite being a lifelong gardener, Mrs Catchpole had overlooked the fact that numerous common plants can be harmful if not treated with respect." Ms Catchpole leaves two children and three grandchildren.

PENNY SAT BACK. "WOW."

"Yeah..." said Izzy softly.

Penny looked at the clock on the wall. "I think I might pop down to the library to see if they have a copy of Sybil's book."

7

Framlingham Library was set back from Market Hill in a building that had once been the town's courthouse. The topmost room, which had once been the court room itself and had beautiful little windows that brought in lots of light, was now often used as an event space or gallery. All the books were downstairs, and the librarians' counter was by the door in a spot which allowed them a commanding view of the ground floor.

The librarian Annalise was staring intently at both her computer screen and a sheet in front of her.

"Checking up on outstanding books?" said Penny as a greeting.

Annalise blinked and looked up. "Do you mean outstanding as in very good, or outstanding as in overdue?"

"Either," said Penny.

"Neither," said Annalise and smiled. She held up the

sheet, which turned out to be the latest edition of the *Frambeat Gazette*. "Any good with cryptic crosswords?"

"No, but always willing to give them a go. I think Izzy was under the impression you were the secret compiler of the weekly crosswords."

Annalise chuckled. "Hardly. I'm no 'Madame Zelda'. No, 'Socrates' is a far cleverer person than me. See, I've got a few. This one: *Welsh songwriting legend: "I loved opera", occasionally,* four letters."

"Welsh songwriting legend. I'd say 'Tom Jones', but it doesn't fit."

"The key bit there is 'occasionally'. It tells us we've got to take the occasional letter from something; in this case, 'I loved opera'. If we take the first letter, skip two, take the next and skip two, we eventually get 'Ivor'."

Penny looked at her blankly.

"Ivor Novello. Welsh songwriter. *We'll Keep the Home Fires Burning.* No?"

"Sorry," said Penny who had never heard of the name.

"That was one of the easy ones."

"Was it? Gosh."

"Look at this one. Twelve across. *Like vermouth, metallic element is a dangerous thing to consume,* nine letters."

"Yes?" said Penny politely.

"This requires the reader to know that sweet vermouth is sometimes called 'it', short for 'Italian'. As in the drink, gin and it."

"I certainly didn't know that."

"Another word for like, if we're being hip, is 'dig'."

Penny thought. "'Dig it', then?"

"Yes. But we've got the metallic element, in this case, aluminium or 'al'. So the first five words can be read as..."

"Dig it al is..." said Penny. "Digitalis."

"Indeed. A substance that is a dangerous thing to consume."

"And people do these for fun?"

"It's more of a compulsion really. But I'm stuck on this one," said Annalise. "*Athena regularly has it, but Hecate always partakes*, three letters. I can't see the simple clue, and I'm thinking that Hecate is goddess of magic and Athena is goddess of beauty..."

Penny frowned. "Tea."

"Pardon?"

"Tea. Is it right?"

"It certainly fits. How did you get that?"

Penny waved a finger at the clue vaguely. "It was sort of there in the letters the two names had in common, and when I saw it I thought 'tea'! That's something some people have regularly, and which some people always partake."

"Ah," said Annalise. "Regularly. The even numbered letters in 'Athena'. Of course." She wrote it in, then seemed to remember herself and looked at Penny. "You didn't just come in to help me solve crosswords, did you?"

"I did not," Penny admitted. "I was wondering if you had a copy of *The Golden Bell* by Sybil Catchpole?"

Annalise held up a finger to indicate she was on the case and came round her desk.

"You don't need to look it up on your database?" said Penny.

"Don't need to. We've always had a couple of copies. She was a local woman – died in the winter."

"Yes, I know."

"And *The Golden Bell* has strong links to the local area. Very local. One of the pictures is clearly of Fram Castle and another is of St Michael's church." She led Penny through to the local history section.

"I assumed a picture book would be among the children's books."

Annalise shook her head. "It might pretend to have a story, but it's a fairly weird one if it has. The book's value, beyond the treasure it points to, is the beautiful detail in its illustrations. Here."

She pulled a volume off a shelf and put it in Penny's hands. The hardback book was thinner than Penny expected. The picture on the cover was of a pastoral scene: golden hazy light pouring over bulging oak trees and green fields to illuminate a knight on horseback with a billowing pennant in his hand. There was something about the illustration that struck Penny as intrinsically seventies. Was it the warm, natural colours? Was it the fact that the style didn't aim for comforting cartoonishness, but was unashamedly and unsettlingly characterful? Whatever it was, the image was entrancing.

"And on the reverse..." said Annalise, encouraging Penny to flip it over.

On the back was another picture, a photograph this time.

"The golden bell," said Penny.

The item, laid on green grass to be photograph, gleamed white, yellow and bronze. Its surface was not smooth but dimpled, and many of those dimples were inset with precious stones.

"There's a solid gold bell still buried out there somewhere?" said Penny.

"Unless someone's already found it and never said," Annalise nodded.

"Crazy."

"It was the seventies. I gather Sybil herself was a bit of a hippie. Saddled her two children with silly names."

"Gwen?"

"Short for Guinevere. She got off more lightly than her brother."

"Barry?" said Penny, not thinking it was a terrible name.

"And I can't say I'm impressed by the names Gwen gave her own children," said Annalise.

Penny frowned and tried to recall. "Mary, Joseph and Donny? Not awful names."

"Think on it. Donny is the youngest."

Penny didn't understand but said nothing.

"Let's get that book checked out for you," said Annalise. "It's time to close soon. And I'll give you a copy of the *Gazette*, see if you can solve any more of those clues." She led the way back to the counter. "For me, there's only one treasure I'm interested in."

"Oh?" said Penny.

Annalise tapped a colourful potato print poster for the Easter egg hunt at Brick Lane copse that had been taped to the screen around the librarian's desk. "Merida and I are going to score big," she said.

Penny thought it was interesting that a woman who had named her own daughter Merida might poke fun at the names other people gave their children, but said nothing.

8

Izzy's dad, Teddy, dropped her around to Marcin's farmhouse in the evening. The little van he used for transporting his mobile disco and karaoke equipment was equally useful for delivering adult daughters and their bags of belongings. As he pulled into the yard, Marcin came out to greet them.

"You have luggage! Let me help you." He shook hands with Izzy's dad. "Mr King! You are coming inside for a drink?"

"No, lad," said Teddy. "I'm doing an Elvis night at the King's Head in Yoxford and I have to get ready."

"I understand. My great-grandmother was a big fan of rock and roll. Elvis, Dean Reed, Czerwono-Czarni."

"Er, I've not heard of them," said Teddy. "I must look them up."

As best as Izzy could understand, her boyfriend's great grandma had also been some sort of underground resistance vigilante during the Second World War. Clearly, she had been a very interesting woman.

Marcin and Izzy waved Teddy off, then he helped Izzy haul her bags inside. Marcin Nowak ran a dog obedience school from this former farm. There was a secured paddock area where dogs, good or bad, could roam and be trained in safety, and around about the place were a number of buildings in various states of disrepair.

"I am very happy that you have brought some things over," said Marcin as they stepped inside. "I will carry them up to the bedroom."

Marcin's three house dogs ran around their feet in happy agreement.

"Wooster! Tibia! Skidoo! Away!" he commanded, smartly but softly, and all three went off at once. Skidoo, a great big lolloping thing, collided with a kitchen chair as he went, but he went nonetheless. Marcin had a supernatural way with animals, although Izzy was amused by his penchant for naming them with zero consideration for the words' meaning in English. She had yet to ask him why he thought Tibia was a good name for a dog.

She looked at her luggage. "Ah – only that little bag needs to go upstairs. The rest are for the dining room."

"Huh. Maybe later you can explain. Come and let us find you some shelf space."

The house was a beautiful stone farmhouse filled with period detail. The staircase was made from oak, and so large that the half landing was spacious enough to house a rug for one of Marcin's dogs, who liked to look out of the window there. Marcin's room had a large wooden wardrobe and a chest of drawers, but one of the house's great features were the built-in cupboards set into the thick walls. It was one of these that Marcin opened.

"I thought that this might be suitable for you. What do you think?"

Izzy was slightly torn. The built-in cupboard was spacious, but there were small crevices around the edges. She pictured insects coming out of the walls and climbing over her clothes. Izzy had no problem with spiders, but clothes moths or destructive beetles were another matter. She eyed the wooden chest of drawers, wishing she could have space in there.

"Um, good. I can just put my bag in there for now, maybe unpack later." Izzy would not be laying things directly on the shelves. She put the holdall in the cupboard and closed the door.

"I should think about our dinner," Marcin declared.

"Aha, no need!" said Izzy. "My mum made an extra nut roast pie so that I could bring one along with me. I will prepare food for tonight."

"I look forward to tasting this unusual delicacy," said Marcin. "Does one have nut roast pie in place of meat?"

"Yes, that is very much the idea. My mum is vegan." Izzy looked at the obvious doubt spreading across Marcin's face. "You're worried about not having meat?"

"Worried is the wrong word. I guess I am curious to see if I will still be hungry after eating nuts."

"There is only one way to find out," said Izzy. "You may stand and watch while I perform wizardry in the kitchen!"

"I can be useful," said Marcin. "I will pour wine so that the cook does not go thirsty."

A few minutes later, Izzy had a glass of wine pushed along the counter as she chopped onions for the tomato sauce to accompany the nut roast.

"Ah, may I make a small, er, comment?" Marcin said. "That is the pastry board, I will find you a chopping board for the onions."

Izzy stood back as Marcin changed over the boards. "What's the difference?"

Marcin gave a shrug as if it was obvious. "I don't want my pastry to taste of onions. Separate boards is good sense. This one for chopping vegetables, and this one for preparing pastry. You were not to know which was which of course, but now you do."

Izzy continued chopping onions with a small shrug. She was an old hand at making tomato sauce as it was ever-present in the King household, and went with everything.

When it was bubbling nicely she turned her attention to vegetables, being sure to prepare them on the correct board. As she sipped her wine she told Marcin about the interesting new commission that she and Penny had to make memory bears, and indeed some tie-dye kaftans as well.

"I think we're just a few minutes away from being ready, would you like to lay the table?" asked Izzy.

"On it!"

Izzy was delighted to see that Marcin had gone all-out and had laid the table with a cloth and napkins. She banished thoughts of putting the food directly onto their plates, and used serving dishes. There was her mum's nut roast pie in a glass dish, Izzy's homemade tomato sauce decanted into a large jug, and a big pile of carrots and broccoli.

Marcin inhaled deeply. The fragrance was winning him over, and Izzy was excited to see if he liked the pie.

"This looks very appetising!" said Marcin as they took their seats. "Oh, but I think maybe you forgot to bring in the potatoes."

"Sorry?"

"It's okay. I can fetch them." He was halfway to his feet when their eyes met and he saw Izzy's confusion. "Ah. Right. There are no potatoes. Perhaps you forgot?"

"Um, no. There is pastry," said Izzy, with a wave of her hand. "The pastry is the carb for this meal. We don't need potatoes."

"Don't need potatoes," Marcin echoed. "Huh."

"Huh?"

He forced a smile. "You have prepared a delicious meal for me and it is not easy working in someone else's kitchen." Those were the words, but his eyes continued to search the table, as if the potatoes had simply been mislaid. "Sorry, why would we not need potatoes?"

"The carbs? Carbohydrates? My mum calls it starch. Anyway, you can have potatoes, bread, maybe pasta, or pastry like we have here. You don't need more than one of those things."

"Is this a rule? That is not a rule." Marcin shook his head and stared hard at Izzy. "I never heard this rule. Who told it to you?"

Izzy was stumped. "I, um, I'm not sure. It's just how things are, isn't it?"

"I don't think so, Izzy. Yes, pasta with a pasta dish. Rice with a rice dish maybe, but meat pie is a potato dish. Pie comes with potatoes."

"That's not a rule either."

He leaned back and breathed deeply as though trying to find some calm. "It is like a shirt and tie," he said.

"Pardon?"

"If you go for a job interview, you must wear a shirt and tie. The potatoes are the tie to the pie's shirt. If you wear the shirt without the tie then something is missing."

"The pastry is the tie," said Izzy.

"I am sure that it is lovely, but I am saying it is not the tie."

"Uh-huh. I am definitely hearing that loud and clear. Still, think of it this way, your next meal with potatoes will be amazing, because you missed them for a day."

Izzy's words of comfort clearly didn't hit home as intended as they ate in silence for some time.

"The pastry is good," he said eventually.

There was an unspoken second part to the sentence. Izzy was quite certain what he really meant (but was too polite to say) was "The pastry is good, but it's not potatoes, is it?" or perhaps "The pastry is good, but I am not keen on the nut roast in place of meat."

It had crossed Izzy's mind that not every household was like the one she came from. Musical evenings where the family played instruments and made riotous amounts of noise were a case in point. She didn't know anybody else who did that.

"What else are we going to find that we don't understand about each other?" She put down her knife and fork. "There are probably loads of things! We should figure out what they are and get them out of the way."

Marcin put his hand on hers. "If we knew what those things were, it wouldn't be a problem. It's the unexpected nature of things that stops us in our tracks, so we must just face them as they come."

"That's easy for you to say," huffed Izzy. "You're not the one who's failed the potato exam."

Marcin roared with sudden laughter. "Ah, this is how we will manage, Izzy! Potato exam! I am sorry for my face betraying me. I was a little shocked, I admit, but I will not die from the lack of potato. At least I hope not."

"Good. Happy to hear it."

"And the nut roast pie is – what can I say? – it's really not as bad as I feared."

"Mum will be thrilled to hear feedback like that," said Izzy. "Thrilled."

He got up, came round the table, took her face in his hands and kissed her on the lips (which would have been much more romantic if she didn't have a mouthful of nut roast). "You are an amazing woman, Izzy. I look forward to finding out all about you."

"Okay, potato boy," she said, waving him away and smiling. "I hope we have lots of time to do that."

9

The sky above the town glowed orange as the sun set. Although there was no summer warmth, Penny was cheered by how the days were growing noticeably longer. She was able to take Monty out for his evening walk after seven o'clock and the sky was still light. There was music in the air, either a choir in the church or a folk band in a pub. It was too distant and distorted to tell.

The Crown was doing a brisk Saturday night trade and a few hardier souls were drinking at the pavement tables. Old McGillicuddy and Timmy were still at their regular seating spot in the middle of the quiet marketplace. One man and his dog watching the clouds go by. Once Monty had sniffed at every doorway around the square, like a nightwatchman doing his rounds, the little corgi was happy to go back inside and join Penny upstairs in her little flat on the top floor.

Penny had spent several years living in London and was used to living in tiny accommodation. However, the rooms she had above Cozy Craft, whilst small, were a comforting little haven and not cramped at all.

Monty had basket beds both in the shop and in Penny's rooms (both constructed by Izzy), and a selection of toys in each. While Penny made herself a fruit zinger herbal tea, Monty arranged, then rearranged the toys in his basket.

"Settled down now?" she asked and climbed into bed with her tea.

She wore a fleecy hoodie over her pyjamas while she sat up in bed. A while back, friend (and at the time potential boyfriend) Aubrey Jones had bought her a thick fluffy housecoat that would have been cosier, but it was a hideously old-fashioned thing that not even the chilliest great grandma would consider wearing. Said would-be boyfriend was now very happily going out with a local GP (a fact which caused Penny only the minutest pangs of bitter self-pity) and she relied on more conventional clothing to keep her warm.

Monty circled in his bed before flopping down, deflating like a punctured football. Penny sipped her tea, realised it was still too hot, and opened the library copy of *The Golden Bell*. There was a foreword from the author on the first page.

To FIND *the fabled golden bell,*
    there is but one thing you should know:
    The wisest will look past the lies to find
    the treasure buried below...

. . .

THIS BOOK CONTAINS *sixteen pictures which tell the story of brave Sir Percival and his search for the golden bell. The pictures feature arcane symbols and imagery which, when correctly deciphered, will provide the exact location of a golden bell I have buried somewhere on public land in England. The bell is decorated with opals and pearls, and has a value at which I can only guess. With a little knowledge of botany, mythology and cartography, any person young or old might be able to solve this puzzle and find the bell.*

S. Catchpole
Avalon Cottage
Suffolk

PENNY THOUGHT either it was only luck that someone hadn't yet found the treasure, or Sybil Catchpole had wildly overestimated the abilities of other people – young or old. If the treasure had lain undiscovered for four decades, it seemed unlikely Penny would be the one to solve it, but she was nonetheless intrigued.

She turned to the first page of the story, and a picture of a castle on a hill, and began to read.

10

"And the story follows this knight, Percival, and his quest," said Penny the following day. "On each page he meets a different person, or is in a different place. It's all wonderfully painted. Very intricate in the way that's sometimes a bit creepy."

"Creepy?" said Izzy.

"The eyes. The eyes follow you."

"Sign of good art, that."

Izzy looked at one of Sybil's paintings on the wall. That morning, after Izzy had been to church, they had come back to Avalon Cottage. They had utilised the key Gwen had loaned them so they could go through the textiles in the house. The painting on the wall was of a garden: the one here, in fact. A sandy-haired child sat in the foreground, back to the artist, but head turned to look directly out of the picture at the viewer. The eyes were piercing. Izzy could see Sybil had been a very gifted artist.

Penny gestured about. "We will leave curtains at all of the windows so the place will still have some privacy. Everything else will go on one of these piles."

Izzy watched as Penny produced printed sheets with huge lettering. The first read To be used for memory bears, the second Needs checking, may be of value, and the third Donate to charity shop or make use of fabric. Penny put each on one of the easy chairs in the lounge.

"Can I suggest a refinement?" said Izzy. "The charity shop pile is likely to be the biggest, so let's put that one on the settee. If we see something we might like to take back to the shop we can put it on the left, and we put the charity shop things on the right."

Penny re-arranged the signs. "Good. Let's get cracking. Where shall we start?"

"Let's get the silky drapes from the bedroom. We know we'll use those for the bears, so we might as well start with something straightforward."

"Good idea. I shared pictures of those with some people in a group I'm a member of, to see if anything might be valuable."

"Any useful feedback?" Izzy asked.

"The gist of it seemed to be they are valuable as lovely fabric; nothing over and above that. We can crack on knowing we're not cutting into antiques or anything."

They went upstairs and started to remove the silk drapes from their positions around the bedroom when Penny paused.

"Did you just hear something downstairs?"

"Yes." Izzy couldn't remember what kind of a lock the

door had. Had they left it open?

The two of them went downstairs to check.

"Hello?" asked Penny.

They came face to face with a man in the lounge. He was perhaps in his late forties, with a ruddy face and sandy hair. He wore wellies and a waxed jacket, and carried a long gadget in his hand that Izzy momentarily mistook for a cordless vacuum cleaner before recognising it as a metal detector.

"What's all this then?" he asked them, gesturing at the signs on the seats. "Are you robbing the place?"

"We'd be very organised robbers if we were sorting stuff before we took it," said Izzy.

"I'm sorry, who are you?" said Penny. She stood tall. Izzy could see that she was determined not to show fear to this intruder.

"You are a stranger in my mother's house. I'll ask the questions," he said tersely.

"You're Gwen's brother," said Penny.

The man nodded. "Twins, yes. Barry. You?"

"Penny, Izzy. From the sewing shop," said Penny. "Gwen gave us a key so that we can help to sort out some of the clothes and soft furnishings. We're going to be making memory bears."

"Memory bears." He looked as if he had no idea what that meant and sighed irritably. "Good that you're doing some clearing out." He shook hands with both of them, brief and formal.

"We're sorry about your mum," said Izzy.

"She was old and pig-headed," said Barry, then seemed to

remember himself. "I mean, thank you. It's always difficult, losing a parent. Very much her own person, she was."

"It's clear that she was a fascinating character," said Penny with a smile. "We should carry on with what we're doing. I was going to put the kettle on in ten minutes or so, if you'll still be around?"

Izzy smiled at Penny's tactful interrogation.

"I'll only be here for five minutes," he said. "I was going to grab mum's collection of old ginger beer bottles. I know an enthusiast who will enjoy them." He nodded at a row of old-fashioned bottles lined up on a high shelf. "'Eyes only' finds aren't to everyone's tastes, but..."

"Oh, they are the ones with a marble in the neck," said Penny. "How lovely!"

"Do you want a box for them?" asked Izzy. "We brought some with us."

"That would be useful, yes."

Izzy produced a box while Barry retrieved the bottles from the shelf.

"'Eyes only finds'?" Penny asked.

He shook the metal detector in his hand. "Can't find everything with one of these. Some treasures you simply have to find by sight alone. Suffolk Searchers Metal Detecting Club is always looking for new members. We meet at the Castle community rooms on Fridays if you're interested."

"Maybe we should wrap those bottles in newspaper so they don't clink together," said Izzy. "I saw some over by the bureau."

She went to the large upright desk in the corner of the

lounge. Every inch of the desk and the shelves stacked above it was covered in papers and pens, notepads – even little jars of paintbrushes for watercolours, now completely dried out.

There was a hardback book on the desktop, red with an embossed gold pattern on the cover. Automatically, Izzy opened it and flicked through. The pages were filled with dense hand-written notes, but it was all complete gibberish. The words were made up of random strings of consonants and vowels that could not possibly belong to any earthly language.

"What's this?" she said.

Barry grunted. "Oh, mum's secret journal."

"What does it say?"

He shrugged. Izzy could see huge indifference in that gesture; he really did not care. "There's a cipher for it at the front."

"Not tempted to decode it now she's gone?"

He rolled his tongue around the inside of his mouth. "Ask yourself this, if you were going to keep a secret journal, would you leave it out in plain sight where any visitor could see it?"

Izzy frowned.

"Answer that and you'll know everything you need to know about my mum."

Izzy made a thoughtful noise, picked up the pile of newspapers from the shelf behind the bureau and brought them over to Barry. They were very old indeed, the top ones dating back to the nineteen eighties.

"Did she collect the special editions, like royal weddings?" Penny asked, peering at them.

Barry didn't reply but took the top one, screwed it up carelessly and jammed it down among the bottles already in the box.

"I can help with that," said Izzy, hoping it didn't sound like "You're doing that wrong."

"You've got things to do, haven't you?" said Barry. He reached for the next newspaper, then froze, hand outstretched.

He was paused in a way that made no sense to Izzy. She was about to ask what was wrong when he jerked back into life, snatched up the box, and with it under one arm and the metal detector in his hand, made for the door.

"Is everything all right?" Penny called.

"Lock up when you're done," he said. "This is my cottage now, you know."

And with that he slammed the door behind him and was gone. Izzy was halfway to following him to the door, but there was no point in following.

"How very, very odd," she said.

"Yes," said Penny. She had the next paper from the pile in her hands. "Look at this."

"What is it?"

Penny passed the paper to her. It took Izzy a moment to find the small article on the page.

"*Drunk driver dies in prison,*" she read. "*A verdict of misadventure was recorded at the inquest into the death of Ivor Catchpole. Although Catchpole (36) had consumed large amounts of a toxic substance, believed to be an alcohol substitute, it was not believed that he had intended to take his own life, the inquest heard. Catchpole died while serving a prison sentence for causing death by dangerous driving."* Izzy looked at the date at the top of the paper. "Nineteen eighty-two. How sad."

"Gwen's dad dying in prison? Or the person he killed with his car?" said Penny.

"All of it," said Izzy. "Gwen said he was an alcoholic."

"Horace next door said that Ivor was an alcoholic. Gwen was less keen to discuss it."

"It sounds as though Sybil's husband – Gwen and Barry's dad – lived a troubled life."

"Everything we find out about this family is either strange or tragic," said Penny.

"We never really know what goes on behind closed doors, do we?"

"True."

"Like potatoes," said Izzy.

"Pardon?"

"Potatoes. You have no idea how strongly another person might feel about potatoes until you cross that line in the sand and then *boom!*"

Penny frowned at her. "Our conversation seems to have drifted. Are we now talking about you and Marcin? How is domestic bliss *chez* King and Nowak?"

"Marcin thinks potatoes and pie go together like a shirt and tie."

"You're saying words, but I'm not following."

Izzy explained Marcin's intransigent viewpoint on the role of potatoes in a dinner.

"I get it," said Penny after she'd finished.

"You do?"

Penny nodded. "I worked in hospitality. You soon learn

that people get mad if a meal doesn't meet their own personal expectations, and that can be very different depending on who you're dealing with."

"I have a bunch of new things to learn," grumbled Izzy. "I wish there was a way to make it easier."

"He has to learn things about you too," said Penny.

"What things?" Izzy asked. "I'm straightforward as they come. There are no surprises here."

Penny gave her one of those looks that appeared to be a friendly smile, but there was a tiny hint of "You just wait and see."

"Back to textiles. We'll do another thirty minutes and see how far we get," said Penny.

When they finished for the day, they surveyed the neat piles they'd created. "I might take some of the drapes and hang them out on the line at Marcin's," said Izzy. "It will get rid of any dust."

Penny nodded. "We'll bag up the charity shop stuff and leave it for Gwen. That just leaves the things which need to be checked out. You're right, though it pains me to say it: Carmella Mountjoy would be best placed to sell on these items, or find them a new home."

"And we can treat it as peace offering," Izzy smiled brightly.

11

I zzy's phone buzzed.

Penny caught sight of Izzy's expression as she read whatever message was on the screen. "What on earth is the matter?"

Izzy put the phone down. "Obviously I wasn't thinking about crazy projects or anything, but I got an update on something I had been following. Quite beyond my control. Anyway, those fleeces are no longer for sale."

"Oh, that is a shame," said Penny.

"You're secretly relieved we won't have grubby fleeces hanging around the shop."

"I didn't say that."

Izzy sighed "It's all part of resisting temptation, I guess. A missed opportunity."

"Do you know what I saw in Wallerton's bakery?" said Penny, clearly trying to cheer her up. "They had biscuits with lambs iced on them for Easter. I know it's no substitute for a fleece, but I could go and get some if it might cheer you up?"

Izzy raised her eyebrows. "Surely that would make me a very shallow individual, if my mood could be altered with a cute sugary snack?"

Penny nodded. "It would make you very human. You can be sad at the missed opportunity but enjoy a short-term boost. Nothing wrong with that."

"Oh, go on then."

THAT EVENING, Izzy returned to Marcin's farmhouse, carrying the drapes from Avalon Cottage in a large black bag. Marcin was on cooking duty, so he greeted her at the door, wearing his apron. Skidoo waited near the doorway, trained not to step over the threshold until invited, but also not wanting Marcin to forget he was there.

Izzy caught a waft of delicious cooking smells. "That smells amazing!" she said.

"I hope it lives up to the promise," said Marcin. "Can I help you with that bag?"

"No, it's some textiles that need to blow in the wind a little bit, get the dust off them," said Izzy. "I'll put them on the line tomorrow, but maybe I'll leave them in the dining room for now?"

"A bag of dirty things does not belong in the dining room."

"They are not exactly dirty, just a bit—" She saw the look on his face. "—Fine. I'll put them in one of the outbuildings."

"I wanted to ask you about the other bags that you left in the dining room," said Marcin. "Where will they go?"

"Those are projects," said Izzy. "For Lent. I am restricting myself to one at a time, so there isn't too much stuff, but the dining table will be so good for cutting and construction. I can't wait to spread my things out."

Marcin maintained a carefully neutral face, but Izzy could almost see the cracks. He had a poker face which served him well, but she had noticed he used it as a mask when he was processing something that he wasn't happy with.

"What?" Izzy asked. "Is something the matter?"

"No, projects are good," said Marcin. "Diversions that take us away from the humdrum should always be applauded. Sometimes, before you came, I would get out a jigsaw."

"Yeah! Similar thing!" Izzy grinned. "Maybe we could share the table? You won't take up much space with a jigsaw."

"The thing is, Izzy, if I had a jigsaw that would take me more than one day, I would roll it up inside a cloth so I could clear the table for my meal."

If Izzy had a soundtrack to her life, it was a bouncy playlist that helped her to boogie through life in her own playful way. Marcin's comment was like one of those filmic moments where the needle *scritched* across the record, stopping the music, and with it the cheerful flow of how Izzy thought life with Marcin was going to be.

"Are you saying the table always gets cleared, even if really interesting things are happening on it? It's a massive table!"

"It is a large table, yes. Mealtimes happen here though, and a calm meal time is an essential thing for well-being. This is true for humans as much as it is for dogs."

Skidoo raised his head at the mention of dogs.

Izzy clamped her mouth shut. Dog training wisdom was Marcin's speciality, and she was in no position to argue with what he'd said.

Marcin checked something in a saucepan, then looked up at Izzy's face. "You have thoughts on this?"

Izzy paced up and down as she processed her thoughts. "Yes. It's taking me a while to get them in order, because there's something I don't understand." She stood still, looking over at him. "You and I both like to do wild and fun things. We both embrace the crazy things, yeah?"

"We do, it's very true. I enjoy the wild and crazy so much more since I met you."

"So, the thing I don't understand is how you can want wild and crazy, but also want the table cleared for mealtimes? You can't embrace the chaos on one hand, then be a neat freak on the other!"

"You express this very well, Izzy, which is helpful. I would perhaps counter your assertion that one has to embrace chaos at the expense of all else."

Izzy pouted. He was going to be all reasonable about this. She felt righteous anger at his betrayal of the weirdo club she'd invented in her head, and now he was taking all the wind out of her sails by being pleasant. "Fine," she sighed with a dramatic eye roll for comic effect. "Let's hear your counter argument."

"We all need balance to be healthy. Energy and chaos is

part of that balance, but sometimes we should be still and calm."

"Is this dogs or humans?" Izzy asked.

Marcin looked at her reproachfully. "I know you understand my meaning. Now, tell me truthfully whether you have ever found enjoyment in putting things in order?"

"Well, yes. Sometimes."

"So between us we must find where the balance is. We will do marvellous chaotic things together, and sometimes we will be tidy. Shall we try this thing out?"

Izzy huffed. "Yes?"

There was a small part of her brain that understood the value of an empty table, but she knew the other part of her brain, the part which wanted to hog the table like a troupe of messy and stubborn chimpanzees, would take some convincing to change its ways.

Who knew living together would be so hard?

"Well, you'll be pleased to know those fleeces I was thinking of buying have been bought up by someone else," she said sniffily. "One less thing to clutter up your home, I suppose."

"Yes, I suppose," said Marcin. It sounded like he really didn't care at all.

12

On Monday, Penny created the palettes for the memory bears. She came up with the idea of putting samples into a notebook which they could give to Gwen on completion. Each page would have samples relating to a particular bear, and she would leave space for Gwen to add details of what she might remember about the fabric. There was even room for photos, if Sybil had been pictured wearing any of them.

"That is very nice," said Izzy, peering over her shoulder.

"Thank you. It's strange when you cut out tiny samples with the pinking shears: all fabrics look amazing."

"It's the neat and tidy thing. You're making a miniature allotment with little fabric plantings. Did I tell you Marcin is trying to tell me that a bit more tidiness in my life will be a good thing?"

"Goodness me! I am intrigued to see how that experiment turns out," said Penny.

"He thinks I might find some unexpected pleasure in putting things in order."

"He might be right," said Penny. "You never know."

"Cute little fabric allotments might be a case in point." Izzy pointed at the notebook. "Although I can't quite see the link between this – which is fun – and tidying away the table at the end of the day – which is not fun."

Penny grinned. "So these memory bears then, do we need a pattern?"

"I don't think it can be that hard," said Izzy. "I've been making some sketches."

"Oh yes?" Penny thought back to some of Izzy's previous attempts at sketching out construction details, but was careful not to mention them. "Can I see?"

Izzy flipped open a sketch pad. "Ignore the first few. I tried doing them like elongated fashion models, but it turns out that teddy bears are not the right shape for that."

Penny looked at the page. Izzy had created some perfectly lovely sketches of teddy bears. "Nice! So how do we transform this into something we can sew?"

"I'll have a go with some calico," said Izzy. "It's just ears on a head, then arms and legs on a body. It should be pretty easy."

An hour later, Izzy had produced a teddy bear. She dropped it in front of Penny.

"What do you think? I decided that I would go with cutesy over-sized ears on a cutesy over-sized head."

Penny turned it over in her hands. "I'm not sure the big ears are working. I can see the idea, but it makes it look more like an elephant, or a mouse."

"No, no," said Izzy. "If it had a face you'd soon see the difference. Let me draw some features onto the calico."

Izzy took the teddy and added eyes, a nose and a mouth using a felt tip. She held it at arm's length to take a good look at it. "Um."

"Yeah," said Penny. "You should definitely avoid wild, staring eyes on our memory bears. It has the look of a soul-sucking zombie mouse now, with teeth apparently. Why have you given it teeth?"

"I thought it would be more true to life," said Izzy.

"True to life if it was for a horror film. No teeth on memory bears."

"I wonder if Sybil wore dentures?" Izzy mused. "We could look—"

"Heaven help us! No!" said Penny. "No teeth on memory bears. Ever. I think we can call that a life rule."

Izzy reached for the seam ripper. "I will re-make it with smaller ears."

"Adjust this bit too," said Penny, taking the bear and leaning on its face so that she could pin some small folds into it. She worked a safety pin into the calico to hold the fold in place, then made a few more adjustments, each one fastened firmly with another safety pin. "See how it looks more like a bear?"

Izzy held it up. "It's a bear with a lot of piercings, I like it! I'll go back and re-work the pattern I made." She sat the bear on top of the till, wearing its safety pins. Monty growled half-heartedly at it.

13

Penny continued to arrange tiny rectangles of fabric in the notebook while Izzy worked on the bear prototype.

"I'm like a fabric gardener, designing which flower should go where," she said thoughtfully.

"You'd enjoy one of those things that quilters use," said Izzy. "They are like a giant Fuzzy Felt board for the wall where you can audition fabrics for a project."

"What? It sounds lovely," said Penny.

"A design wall. We could make one," said Izzy.

Penny was about to demand more detail when the shop door opened and Carmella Mountjoy strode in.

The mood in the shop plummeted. Carmella had a way of bringing her own personal storm cloud of negative energy into a room. The middle-aged woman was tall and slender and should have moved with the elegance of a swan, yet entered with the emotional stiffness of a bundle of sticks.

"Good morning, Carmella. How can we help you today?" said Penny with an overly cheerful smile. She was determined Carmella would not intimidate them with her brittle manner and disdainful scowl.

"It turns out you have already been 'helping' me." She gave the air quotes heavy amounts of weighty sarcasm. "I just came to find out what it is that you're up to."

"Um, what?" said Izzy.

"Would you like to explain?" Penny asked.

"What I mean is that someone came into my shop with some vintage garments, claiming you had sent them there." She raised her eyebrows as if that was sufficient evidence of wrongdoing.

"Er, yes," said Izzy.

"So what is your angle?"

"Angle?"

"Are they stolen perhaps? Did you infect them with smallpox? What?"

Penny walked round to face her directly. "Mrs Mountjoy, have you just accused us of waging biological war upon your shop?"

"You know what I mean!"

"I'm sure I don't. Where is this coming from?"

"I know your tricks!"

"It's only you that sees us as competitors. We don't deal in vintage clothing, which is why we sent Gwen along to you."

"I see how you're playing it," Carmella spat, jabbing a finger at Penny. "It's your little miss goody-two-shoes act again."

"We were trying to help a customer solve a problem. We

thought she would be in safe hands. I do hope you weren't rude to her, just because she mentioned our names?"

Carmella wasn't even paying attention. She stared at the till and pointed a quivering finger. "Is that supposed to be me?"

"Eh?" Penny was having trouble keeping up with Carmella's ranting.

Carmella held up the teddy bear with its safety pins.

"This! You've made some kind of effigy of me, and you've stuck pins in it!"

Penny really didn't know what to say. Izzy clamped her hand to her mouth, made a little suppressed squeal, then let out the laughter she couldn't hold in.

"Ha!" Carmella crowed, finger pointing at Izzy. "Guilt! I've been having these tension headaches and now I know why. You and your voodoo dolls!"

Penny felt her patience slipping away. "Carmella, there is so much wrong with what you're saying."

"Not least that so-called voodoo dolls aren't part of the voodoo religion," said Izzy. "I did a 'Word Nerd' column on it."

"Done your research, eh?" said Carmella.

"Do you think it looks like you?" asked Penny.

Carmella regarded the teddy, her expression shifting as she realised she'd possibly spoken foolishly. "It could be anything, really. It's the intention that counts though. If you intend it to cause me harm then the likeness probably doesn't matter."

Izzy slipped out of her chair and joined Penny. "Carmella,

here's the thing. You think we think about you all the time, but we really don't. Maybe you think about us all the time? We think about you ... hardly ever. This thing is a teddy prototype. It was hard to get it looking right because we didn't base it on an actual real teddy. If we want to make wicked witches for Halloween, maybe we *will* base it on you."

Carmella gave a frustrated roar of annoyance and threw the teddy onto the counter. "You two are the limit. You must stop undermining me!"

She strode out of the shop, banging the door as she went.

"Proper flouncing that was," said Izzy. "Did you see her? I think there were even tears in her eyes."

"Yes," sighed Penny. "What on earth is the matter with her?"

"Dunno," said Izzy. "But one good thing came from her visit. We've got a name for the teddy-that-went-wrong." She held up the calico bear. "Meet our new pincushion, Carmella!"

"Izzy!"

Monty gave a yip. Whether it was in agreement with Penny's admonishment or in annoyance at having his mid-morning snooze interrupted by the shouty woman was hard to tell.

After that crazed outburst, the shop seemed very quiet indeed. On her lunchbreak, Penny took a fresh look at the *Frambeat Gazette* crossword. Such puzzles were rarely her thing, but since Izzy had made a start and Annalise at the library had given her some help, she had somewhat got into it. Also, with letters from finished clues, it was getting easier.

Four down, *Naval officer is on dangerous substance* might have thrown her, but she had 'P' as first letter and 'N' as the last. It was easy to see that the word was going to be 'poison' – a dangerous substance – and it did not take her long to work out 'PO' came from 'petty officer': a naval rank.

The clue for ten down was *Stress about papers? There's not much you can do about it.* She discovered, with a little internet searching, that 'papers' or 'documents' was often crossword code for 'ID'. Only when she'd realised that stress could also mean a stress in language, or an accent, did she wrap the word 'accent' around 'id' to give 'accident' as the answer. A thing which indeed you can't do much about.

Six across gave her pause for thought. *Killer puzzle? Nothing grand, even if it is the wrong way round.* Eight letters. The first letter was an 'F' and the fourth a 'G', and Penny couldn't help but think it was going to be 'finger'-something, but she just couldn't see it.

"You're very quiet over there," said Izzy as she continued to work on the teddy prototype.

"This crossword," Penny muttered. "Killer puzzle. Killer puzzle?"

"They are a bit," said Izzy. "That Socrates person is too clever for me by half. I'm always foxed by them in the end. Not sure I've ever finished one."

Penny huffed and, despite her earlier success, found herself incensed by the puzzle. How could people do these for fun? Either you knew the answers or you didn't. If you didn't, then the exercise ended in failure. It was like sitting an exam just for the entertainment value.

"It's defeated me," she said, putting the newspaper and pencil down with some force.

"Very good," said Izzy. "So perhaps you'd like to pick up your tools and actually help me do the work we're getting paid for, Miss Slipper?"

Izzy chided her with such a light tone that Penny couldn't help but smile.

14

Izzy returned to Marcin's farm that evening in a buoyant mood. She hadn't quite cracked the prototype teddy, but she had derived so much fun from her poor first attempt that she really didn't mind.

"Good evening!" she called as she found him in the kitchen. He was stirring something on the stove that smelled both sharp and savoury at the same time. Did it have apples in it, perhaps?

"How was your day?" he asked.

They exchanged stories. Marcin had a new client for dog training. He was using the placid and smart nature of Tibia to help him socialise a nervous young setter. Izzy told him about Carmella's visit.

"That woman is a little unbalanced, I think," he said with a shake of his head.

"I went for a walk after she left, said Izzy. "You will never guess what I found in the charity shop!"

"You are correct, I will never guess."

Izzy whipped the book out from behind her. "Check this out. *Fifty ways with potatoes.* Now I can expand my potato repertoire!"

"This is a great book!" said Marcin, flipping through the pages.

"I know, right! What shall we try first? I can cook tomorrow."

"Ah, tomorrow." Marcin lifted a finger. "I am taking a trip, so I will be back rather late."

"A trip? Where to?" Izzy asked.

"I am going to Wales."

"Wales?" Izzy was intrigued. "That is a long way to go for dog training."

Marcin nodded. Izzy waited for him to offer further explanation, but he bent to the saucepan, his face set in concentration.

"Fine," she said as her phone began to buzz. "I will be sure to find a potato recipe that re-heats well." She answered her phone.

"Foxglove!" Penny almost shouted down the phone at her.

"Pardon?" said Izzy.

"Foxglove! Fox! Glove!"

Izzy frowned. "Are you having a medical emergency? Is this some sort of code?"

Penny tutted audibly on the line. *"You said it yourself. Killer puzzle. To puzzle is to fox. The answer to the clue is 'foxglove'."*

"I'm sorry, I don't follow..."

"Nothing grand even if it's the wrong way round. Nothing in

tennis is 'love'; grand gives us 'g'. Move them round and you get glove. Foxglove. The killer in the killer puzzle!"

Izzy took a slow breath. "It's nice that you're getting excited by word-based puzzles, Penny…"

"Foxglove killed Sybil."

"Ah, I see. A coincidence."

"No, it's not," Penny said fiercely. *"I have so much to tell you. Does Marcin drive?"*

"You know he does."

Izzy was looking at Marcin. Marcin, wooden spoon in hand, was looking back at her, puzzled.

"Please, come quick," said Penny. *"The pair of you. Pick me up."*

"Where are we going?" said Izzy.

"Avalon Cottage."

"Why?"

"Because Sybil Catchpole was murdered!"

15

Izzy wasn't sure she had ever properly told Marcin that she loved him. If she hadn't, she was sure she did, nonetheless. And one of the reasons she loved him was when she told him that mad cousin Penny wanted them to pick her up and take her to a cottage on the edge of town, Marcin simply turned off the bubbling dinner on the hob and went to get his car keys without further question.

Only when they were trundling through the gloaming into town did he ask.

"She seems to think our client's mother was murdered," said Izzy.

"Why does she think that?" he said.

"Her death was admittedly unusual but— There she is."

Penny was on the pavement outside Cozy Craft, almost hopping from one foot to another with impatience.

She quickly got into the back of the car. "Thank you. Avalon Cottage, driver, and don't spare the horses."

"Spare what horses?" said Marcin.

"It's an idiom," said Izzy. "Which is one letter away from what my cousin is for dragging us out on a wild goose chase because of a crossword."

"No, listen to this one," said Penny as Marcin pulled away. "One down, *Hide hides hide of opossum with heads of Indian Cobras: it's a serious offence.* Eight letters. I'll be honest, I had to turn to the internet for help again. 'Hide hides' means that we're going to put something inside the word 'hide', and the thing we're going to hide in it is the hide of opossum, as in the outside letters. Put 'o' and 'm' inside 'hide', right?"

"Are you speaking English, Penny?" Marcin asked.

"It's crossword speak," said Izzy. "Doesn't mean Penny hasn't gone completely do-lally, though."

Penny shushed them both. "The heads of India Cobras is 'ic', so put that in there too and you've got 'h' from 'hide', 'om' from opossum, the 'ic', and the rest of 'hide'. Homicide! A serious offence."

"Okay..." said Izzy.

"And this last one. Oh, I had three of the letters anyway. *At first she's impressed but you ultimately fail – she'll have foreseen it all.* 'At first' means we look at the first letters. She's impressed but you. 'SIBY'. Add on the final – ultimate – letter of fail and you get 'Sybil', a prophetess who foresaw things."

"I mean, that sounds right enough," said Izzy kindly.

"Come on! And look at some of these other answers. Digitalis. That's the Latin name for foxglove. Poison. Garden. Botanical. Accident. Tea, for goodness sake! Ivor – that's Sybil's husband's name. Garden Foxglove Poison Tea Homicide Sybil."

Marcin turned up the lane to Avalon Cottage when Izzy pointed. The trees in the surrounding area added a depth to the deepening evening. Izzy could see lights on at Horace and Alison Atkinson's house next door through the trees.

"So," said Izzy slowly – slow because she was not only thinking it through herself, but also wanted to bring a note of calm to proceedings. "You're saying the clues in the *Frambeat Gazette* crossword are telling you that Sybil Catchpole was murdered?"

"It's not the clues telling me, obviously," said Penny irritably.

"Obviously?"

"It's not like I'm divining truths in tea leaves. It's not like the flipping horoscopes you make up for the paper each week."

"Madame Zelda makes them up?" said Marcin, surprised.

Penny huffed. "I'm saying that the crossword compiler knows Sybil was murdered and is telling the world through the medium of the crossword."

Marcin pulled up in front of the house. Penny was out of the car at once and marching to the front door. Izzy could see she had the keys in her hands already.

"Okay! Okay!" said Izzy. "Slow down."

Penny whirled on the stone strewn pathway. "What?"

"I've got—" Izzy counted on her fingers. "—I've got three things to say to you."

"What are they?"

"Okay. Number one, just slow down."

"You've said that."

"Slow down and take a few calming breaths, huh? Two,

can I point out I'm not happy with this role reversal. It's usually you telling me not to get over-excited about something and go off in a mad frenzy."

"I'd hardly call it a frenzy."

Izzy gave her cousin her sternest look, although in truth she wasn't very good at them. "Thirdly, pareidolia."

"Huh?"

"Big posh 'Word Nerd' word. It means that thing humans do when they spot patterns where there aren't any. You've shared with me a bunch of clues from the crossword, but not all of them. There are other words in there. You've focused on the ones which mean something to you."

"Oh, come on. It says Sybil and Ivor. It literally names the method by which she died."

Izzy tilted her head. "Fair enough. So I present to you possible solutions to that, the first of which is that the crossword compiler, Socrates, a local, might have been thinking about Sybil, even subconsciously, while coming up with clues. Things in the back of our minds just seep through."

"What? At least seven or eight clues? Direct links to her death?"

"Okay," Izzy admitted. "So, the crossword compiler was thinking about it consciously. Maybe they do think Sybil was murdered – although I should point out you have both the words 'homicide' and 'accident' in there too. Creating clues about it doesn't equal proof."

"Or maybe it's guilt," said Penny.

Izzy laughed despite the grim subject matter. "She was

killed by Socrates? The crossword compiler did it, and is now confessing to the world?"

"I don't know. Point is – and by the way, you said you had three things to tell me and we're on like number seven already – point is, we thought there was something strange about Sybil's death from the beginning."

"Strange does not have to mean murder."

"I'm surrounded by puzzles and I need answers," said Penny.

"I think you need a soothing hot drink and an early night."

"I had a soothing hot drink, thank you. A fruit zinger."

"Hmmm. Too much zing, I suspect."

Penny turned to the door and put the key in the lock. "I just need—"

"What?" said Izzy.

"I just need to find some answers. Okay?"

"And if the Atkinsons or one of the Catchpole children come and find us here after dark?"

Penny shrugged. "Gwen said we could come and go as we pleased."

"Dressmakers on the night shift, huh?"

"Ours is a mysterious craft and no one knows what we do," said Penny and went inside.

Izzy could do nothing but follow with a backward wave to Marcin as he waited patiently in the car.

———

16

"So, to be clear," Izzy said to Penny in the lounge of Avalon Cottage, "we now think that Sybil was murdered."

Penny didn't like Izzy's tone, not because it was condemning or mocking or superior; it was none of these things. She didn't like Izzy's tone because it was honest and engaged and it forced Penny to critically reflect on her own thoughts.

"Sybil died from drinking tea made with dried foxglove," said Penny. "Doing it accidentally would be an odd death for such an experienced gardener."

"Though not impossible," said Izzy.

"And murder or not, as you rightly point out, the writer of that crossword thinks it's odd enough to write about it in this week's clues."

"Socrates sent us lots of crosswords. This one just happens to have gone in the paper this week."

"Point is," said Penny, thinking there was surely a point to her sudden and powerful suspicions, "Sybil's death has unanswered questions hanging over it. And let's not forget she made and buried a golden treasure worth thousands of pounds somewhere. That could be motive enough in itself."

Izzy's face screwed up. "Really? If someone found the treasure then it's theirs. That's the point of the treasure hunt. You don't need to kill someone to keep it."

"But ... but what if they wanted to know where it was and demanded Sybil tell them?"

"Poisoning as a form of torture? An inducement? That doesn't make sense either."

"Fine. The point is that weird stuff is going on."

"It certainly is. We're standing in a dead woman's cottage after nightfall. That's weird." Izzy turned on a patterned table lamp. "You want to search for clues or something? Not tempted to just phone the police?"

"What? Call up Detective Sergeant Chang at Woodbridge police station? And tell him what exactly? That I did a crossword and now have a *funny feeling*?"

Izzy smiled. "The police would take, er, an objective view of it, yes." She stepped over to the pile of newspapers she had dug out to wrap Barry's bottles in. She slapped a hand on them. "Barry was unpleasantly surprised to see that article about his dad in here."

"You think he didn't know?"

"More of an emotional surprise," said Izzy. "A reminder from his past. He strikes me as an odd fish. Hardly seemed moved by his mother's death. If anything, more interested in shifting some of his mum's old things."

"His parting words to us were that this was his house now. Along with Gwen, he's looking to inherit."

"It's a motive," Izzy nodded. "An older relative who is being too slow to shuffle off this mortal coil."

"I wonder why Sybil kept all those papers?" said Penny. "Is it full of stories about her dead husband?"

"We can take them with us," said Izzy, giving Penny a meaningful look. "If that will get us out of here and allow you to step back and think on things a little more clearly."

"Hang on," said Penny and went over to the bureau. The red and gold journal was still there. She flicked through the pages and pages of handwritten gibberish, then turned to the front page.

There was an inscription which read: "*The secrets of my diaries can be read by simple application of the key below.*" Underneath that was a grid box, with all the letters of the alphabet in order on the first row and a jumble of letters in the boxes underneath.

"More puzzles," said Penny. "Take this."

Izzy reluctantly took the journal. "We are *borrowing* this and returning it at the soonest opportunity," she said, firmly.

"Of course."

Swiftly, Penny rooted through the papers on the bureau shelves. There were a number of unopened letters. They looked like bills, and as the envelopes were still sealed she was unwilling to open them. Given time to think she might have questioned why she felt okay taking a personal journal (coded or not) but felt moral qualms about ripping open impersonal financial mail.

"Hey, look at this," said Izzy. She had found a tatty spiral-bound notepad on a furniture unit at the base of the bookcases. From within it she pulled out a green slip of paper.

"What is it?" said Penny.

"A prescription. I guess Sybil never collected it." She brought it closer to the lamplight to better read it. "*Imatinib.* What's that?"

"I don't know," said Penny. "Bring it."

"I'm not stealing an old woman's prescription." She put it down, took out her phone and took a photo of it instead. "Right. We're leaving."

"We haven't finished," said Penny.

Izzy picked up the stack of newspapers. "We've got her newspapers and her secret journal written in code. I'd say that's enough for one night."

Penny seethed, but her cousin was right. They turned out the light, went out, locked up, and returned to the car. Izzy put their haul on the back seat next to Penny before getting in the front.

Marcin looked at the stacks of books and newspapers, frowning. "Are you two burglars?" he asked.

"You'll visit me in prison, won't you?" said Izzy, patting him on the knee.

17

When she entered the shop the next morning, Izzy saw Penny had made a row of the calico teddy bears on the counter in Cozy Craft. She couldn't help but think it looked like one of those illustrations depicting the evolution of man.

First in line the zombie mouse bear, still sporting safety pins in its face, crouched like man's ape-like ancestral forebears. Next came something with smaller ears and a more fully formed face, but its proportions were all wrong. It had elongated limbs like a beanbag frog. Finally, the last bear was the homo sapiens of the evolutionary line. It looked like a loveable keepsake, sitting on its hind legs, with forearms that reached out, asking for a hug. Izzy had drawn on eyes, which gave it an admittedly crazed look, but she tried to look past that and imagine how the bear would look with buttons as eyes.

"That one actually looks good," said Penny, coming

through from the back. "If we use it as a template we can follow it to make the rest of the bears."

"Yes. Carmella can go back on the till, and we'll give that other weird looking one to Monty as a toy, shall we?"

Monty gave a soft whine, but Penny shushed him. "He would love that, I'm sure. Are we going to refer to the pincushion one as Carmella out loud? Eventually one of us will say it in front of the wrong person, and we'll be in trouble."

Izzy grunted. "You, Penny Slipper, are not the arbiter of what we should and shouldn't do."

The pile of papers taken from Sybil's cottage awaited their attention in the workshop upstairs. Izzy was still giving her cousin plenty of reproachful looks regarding last night's jaunt to Avalon Cottage, and wondered when Penny might look through the piles of papers and agree to take them back.

"Let's think about how we will make these bears," said Izzy. "Some of the fabrics we have will be fine to use as they are, although we should back them with interfacing. These silky ones might look lovely if we gathered sections of them into pleated panels and mounted them on top of a sturdy fabric underneath. It would let us retain something of the texture of these finer fabrics."

"Oh, I think I see what you mean. Would that work all over the bear?"

"Let's have a play. It might be suitable for smaller areas only; maybe the paws. A mixture could look very nice."

"So nice that we can start to make them now. Do you want to see some suggestions I have in the notebook? I can move them around; they're not stuck in place yet."

They pored over Penny's palettes.

"When we talked about Houseplant Jungle Bear we were thinking of the green and brown fabrics," said Penny. "You know Judith Conklin in our 'stitch and natter' group made that crazy patchwork handbag. I wondered if we could go further with that one – maybe embroider some leaves across the joins in the fabric?"

"Oh yes! What's that plant with the big leaves that has a name like monster?"

"Monstera?" Penny asked. "Is that the same as a Swiss cheese plant?"

"Those leaves are so bold and recognisable. We could cut out a shape and appliqué it on, perhaps.

Penny added some ideas to the page. "Good. Sounds as if that's in hand. Let's look at Autumn Leaf Bear."

"We can use some of those same ideas for that one, but the palette will be the golden browns and orangey colours you've selected," said Izzy.

"Oh nice. We can take one each and learn from each other," said Penny with a grin.

Izzy tapped the page as they looked over the palettes for Peacock Bear and Moroccan Souk Bear. "You know what we should think about for these two? They are both going to be quite lavish things. Peacock Bear will make use of the velvets and silks in those amazing jewel colours. I wonder if Sybil had any beads or brooches we might add on as little extra bits of decoration."

"Ooh yes." Penny scribbled more notes onto the pages.

Izzy returned to the farmhouse that evening, realising straightaway that Marcin was no longer at home. His van was gone, but so too was the spark of life he brought to the farmhouse.

She let herself in, wondering which of the dogs might have gone with him. She gave a small whistle to see who responded, and was surprised when all three appeared.

"Hello you lovely lot!" She fussed raffish little Wooster, calm Heinz 57 variety mutt Tibia, and gentle giant Skidoo before letting them out for a run in the garden. Obviously whatever kind of dog training Marcin was doing in Wales, it wasn't the kind requiring a canine helper. She would take them all out for a proper walk later.

Izzy pottered around, even scooping up and sorting the laundry, before she realised she was filling the time she would have otherwise spent chatting to Marcin. She went to take clean towels out and put them in the bathroom, but paused as she looked in the airing cupboard, slightly unsure of herself. There was clearly a pile of blue towels, and a pile of brown towels. They were carefully segregated, but what did it mean? She should probably replace the towels she'd put in the wash with similar coloured ones, but now she couldn't remember what they were.

"Flipping heck. Who knew it was going to be so hard, living with someone?"

If she was Penny she would probably have made a list or set of instructions by now. She grabbed some blue towels and put them in the bathroom. She had a fifty-fifty chance of being correct.

18

I zzy was fast asleep when Marcin returned from his travels that night, and when she awoke the next day he was already up, only a warm dent in his side of the bed indicating the place he had lain.

She wandered through the house, calling his name, but he was nowhere to be found. Probably out with the dogs, she assumed. Izzy got herself ready for the day, went to the laundry room in one of the outbuildings to put a load of washing on, then headed into town for work.

Penny was making a start on preparing pieces for two of the memory bears. She had volunteered to interface and cut out the main pieces for Autumn Leaf and Houseplant Jungle Bears so Izzy could look into the tie-dye kaftans. Penny had a production line going with a pile of Sybil's fabric, while Izzy looked up some ideas and techniques on the internet.

"It's interesting how these kaftans from the seventies are

all single coloured," Izzy mused. "Lots of modern pieces use multiple, clashy colours."

"Yeah? Interesting – considering the seventies were not known for understatement," said Penny.

"I think it might be one of those things where it's easier to accomplish complex mixtures and patterns now, with kits and so on."

Penny caught Izzy's meaning. "Is this one of those things where just because you *can* include all of the colours, doesn't necessarily mean that you *should*?"

"Yeah, maybe. Anyway, we should be true to the period. First I will look at the kaftans, then the dyeing."

"Don't dye, Izzy!" said Penny, clutching her imaginary pearls in the most theatrical manner she could muster.

Izzy rolled her eyes, grabbed one of the prototype teddies, and went over to where Penny was working. "No more puns, Penny," she said as she waggled it in Penny's face. "I can't bear it!"

Penny winced, as though physically wounded by the awful wordplay.

There was an April shower just before lunchtime: a hearty but not heavy bit of rainfall against an otherwise clear sky. Izzy wondered if there might be a rainbow somewhere. When the rain had passed, Penny went out to take Monty for his midday walk and to pick up sandwiches for their lunch from Wallerton's bakery. Izzy put the kettle on for a cup of tea in preparation for Penny's return, and as she waited for it to boil, went through to the workshop.

The stack of newspapers from Avalon Cottage still stood there on one of the workshop benches, a guilty reminder.

Izzy wished they didn't have them here, but was also drawn to them.

She leafed through the pile, putting each newspaper aside after a cursory glance. She soon saw that each of them did indeed have a personal link to Sybil. The oldest, from nineteen seventy-eight, had feature articles about Sybil Catchpole and the phenomenal success of her book, *The Golden Bell*. There was a black and white image of young Sybil, not even thirty years old, holding a copy of her book in what was clearly the garden of Avalon Cottage. It was a national paper too. The woman had achieved genuine fame for a time.

Two papers down it was a very different story from only a year later.

Treasure seeker killed by drunk driver

A MAN who died after being hit by a drunk driver just days before Christmas has been named.

Ken Bickerthwaite (29) was struck by a car driven at speed on a track off Brook Lane in Framlingham. Mr Bickerthwaite was pronounced dead at the scene. Mr Ivor Catchpole, a local resident, was arrested and has since been charged with causing death by dangerous driving.

It is understood that Mr Bickerthwaite, who lived in Leicester, was in the area looking for the golden treasure buried in the area by Mrs Catchpole and made famous in her book, The Golden Bell.

Mr Catchpole appeared before Woodbridge magistrates and the matter has been referred to the crown court for trial.

"CRIKEY," whispered Izzy, solemnly placing the paper aside before moving on through the pile. The stories she found in that cursory look featured several about *The Golden Bell* and Sybil's career as an artist, and several about the tragic incidents surrounding the car crash and her husband's subsequent imprisonment. As time went on, the former diminished and the latter increased. It was only an impression, but it struck Izzy that Sybil's fame went into steep decline as both she and her book became intrinsically linked with Ken Bickerthwaite's death.

"Strange and tragic," she said, recalling Penny's words.

Putting the last paper aside, she saw they'd brought Sybil's spiral bound notepad home with them: the one in which the prescription had been tucked. Unlike the coded red and gold journal this notebook was untidy, but legibly English. Izzy flipped through it. There were shopping lists and phone numbers, and scribbled notes with many crossings out. Then Izzy came across something which made her pause in surprise. It took her a moment to work out what it was, and a moment longer to realise how truly impossible it was.

There was the faint jangle of the shop door below.

"We're back!" Penny called. "I've got you chicken mayo salad."

Izzy re-read the lines before her, then followed them onto the next page. It was impossible.

She hurried downstairs, nearly tripping on the bottom step in her hurry.

"Hungry, huh?" said Penny, putting the paper bags of sandwiches on the counter.

"Look! Look!" said Izzy, holding up the notepad for Penny to see. She tapped a line which read:

HOMICIDE: Serious crime? ~~Murderous smuggler~~ *Hide* <u>hides</u> <u>hide</u> *of opossum with – (IC?) heads of Indian cobras? Heart of tropicbird?*

Penny looked at it, frowning. "Wait. That's one of the crossword clues, isn't it?"

"Yes, it is."

Penny reached out and touched the edge of the notepad.

"We took this from Sybil's house," said Izzy.

Penny's frowned deepened. "So, she— Wait. Hang on."

"I know!" said Izzy.

Penny shook her head. "I don't understand."

"You thought the crossword compiler Socrates knew Sybil had been murdered."

"But..."

"Sybil Catchpole *is* Socrates! We know she loved puzzles. She wrote the crossword! It was her all along."

"No. That can't be. She predicted her own murder? That's impossible."

"I know!"

19

Back home at the farm in the early evening, Izzy went to the laundry room to remove and hang the washing. Halfway across the yard, she halted. There was an odd clanking sound coming from somewhere.

"Oh, please don't be broken!" Izzy was mortified at the idea she might have messed up the washing machine. She didn't consider herself an advanced user of white goods, but surely she couldn't have broken it just by putting a load of laundry in?

She went in to find the washing machine silent. The load from the morning was finished. The clanking, wherever it had come from, had stopped. She removed the things and hung them up on drying racks.

A moment later there were arms wrapped around her from behind and a kiss planted on the side of the neck.

"Afternoon!" said Marcin. "I am sorry that I missed you last night."

"And this morning," she said, turning in his embrace and kissing him back. "You were out early."

"Work. I see you washed the dogs' towels. Thank you."

Izzy looked at Marcin, then back at the towels. She didn't know where to start. "Dog towels? I used those to dry myself when I come out of the shower."

"No!" Marcin backed away to give room for his belly laugh. "I should have mentioned this, I am sorry. When I buy new towels, the old ones are for the dogs. At the moment, mine are blue and the ones for the dogs are grey. We should find a colour for yours."

"Mine?" Izzy said confused. "Don't we just grab a towel? Like, whatever's there?"

"The sharing of towels is not always wise," said Marcin. "We can each have our own."

Izzy's world once more tilted slightly. She came from a household where any towel would do. It was understandable that dogs and humans would not share towels, but she had never imagined there would be a problem with humans sharing them.

"Right. Oh hey, listen. There was a weird clanking noise just now. I think it might have been coming from the barn or somewhere."

"Oh right. I will check it out. You should stay out of there in case there's a problem."

Izzy laughed. "What kind of problem might it be? Warring terminators?"

Marcin didn't laugh and the smile fell from Izzy's face. There was a lot she didn't know about farmhouses, but she trusted herself to not go jumping into a threshing machine.

Probably. Assuming she would recognise a threshing machine if she saw one. What could be so harmful that she couldn't go and take a look?

"How was your day?" he asked.

"Busy," she said. "Sold some fabrics to a local dressmaker. Worked on those teddy bears. Oh – Penny thinks that the woman whose cottage you took us to was murdered and left a secret message predicting her own murder in a crossword."

"You have a very busy life," he smiled. "It is hard to keep up with you sometimes."

"Oh, it's surprising what goes on inside people's private lives," she said, deliberately avoiding looking toward the barn.

THE FOLLOWING MORNING, Izzy waited until Marcin was busy with the dogs' breakfast meals before she departed for work. She left the house; but instead of walking directly down to the road, she went round to the barn instead. She approached the large double doors in the old but sturdy brick building. They were padlocked. The doors were old and in need of paint, but the padlock was newer. Perhaps even brand new.

"Huh."

Why on earth had Marcin locked her out? Her imagination shot off in several different directions.

She knocked on the door. "Hello?" she called.

The very act of listening carefully for an answer made

Izzy ashamed of herself. Had she really leapt straight to *imprisoned mad auntie* or *secret wife and children*?

She crept away, hoping he hadn't seen her checking, still burning with curiosity to know what was in the locked barn.

PENNY WAS ABSORBED in the preparation for the bears for most of the morning. Izzy worked on the kaftans.

"Each kaftan is a really simple folded rectangle. Three metres of narrow width cotton, folded over at the top with a quick seam to make the sides. Not all the way up, obviously, as the arms need to come out. The only complicated part is cutting the hole for the head to come through. I might make a facing for that."

"Oh right, that sounds good. I assume we start with plain white cotton?"

"Yep. Then there's the dye and of course our labour. Here you go, I made a quote. You get in touch with Gwen, and meanwhile I will make a kaftan."

"What? Why would you start on that before we've got the go ahead?" asked Penny.

"Because now I can't rest until I have made a tie-dye kaftan," said Izzy, as if it was the most obvious thing in the world.

Penny rolled her eyes and picked up her phone as Izzy cut herself a length of white cotton fabric.

"Good news!" she said a few minutes later. "Gwen has said yes to the quote for the kaftans, so you are doing actual, profitable work."

"Huh. I might just have to make a spare, so I can have one for myself," said Izzy with a wink.

She had found a reference picture, and soon created a garment matching the shape of the original. She put it on over her head and wafted about the shop, swishing the sides. "Ooh, the drama! I can imagine these are lovely to wear when it's really hot. It's perfect to show off a massive pattern as well."

Izzy pulled the kaftan off over her head and smoothed it out on the cutting table. "I'll order some dye. By the time it gets here I'll have all of the kaftans made and ready to go. To get a nice regular pattern I can bunch it up in pleats across the width, then tie it up in sections with string." She demonstrated what she meant, trussing the kaftan into a long sausage of fabric.

Penny watched as Izzy's gaze roamed around the shop. "I can read your mind, you know!" she said.

"Eh?"

"You're just wondering what else might be lying around that could be spruced up with some tie dye."

"You could tell that, just from my face?" said Izzy, incredulous.

"It's more like I know the things that appeal to you. And this one has created that gleam in your eye."

Izzy beamed. "That's settled then. I will order some dye, and we will find more things that need a new treatment." She looked at the clock on the wall. "What do we fancy for lunch today?"

Penny shook her head. "We have a lunch appointment. Well, I do. You're welcome to come along, too."

"We do?"

"With Denise Upton."

"Doctor Denise?"

"The same."

"I didn't know you were friends," said Izzy. "In fact, I thought—"

Izzy didn't finish. For nearly a year, local decorator and handyman Aubrey Jones had been a surprisingly regular visitor to Cozy Craft; always finding a reason to drop in. And the reason had not been hard to spot. He had a soft spot for Penny, and she for him. If she hadn't dithered over whether she wanted a committed boyfriend in her life, and crucially, hadn't invited the wrong man to be her plus one at a wedding at the beginning of the year, then Dr Denise Upton wouldn't have swooped in and made her own play for Aubrey's affections.

"We're not exactly friends, but she's certainly friendly. And I said I wanted to pick her brains over a medical matter."

"Oh?" said Izzy. She was about to ask why when it struck her. "Imatinib."

"That and more besides."

"Then I shall come to keep you out of trouble."

20

Penny put on Monty's lead, locked up the shop, and left a BACK IN AN HOUR sign on the door. Together, she and Izzy walked towards a café just down from the castle on the hill. Daffodils were out in the green spaces of the town, and Easter decorations could be seen in many of the shop windows. The hardware store had a little family of bunnies in the window, although what bunnies thought they were doing with human-sized shears and boxes of weedkiller was anybody's guess.

The café occupied one half of a grand square building that had once been a working men's club. The place was popular, often crowded, the walls filled with antique ornaments and unusual wall art which added to the crowded feel.

Denise Upton, far younger and seeming far brighter eyed than one might normally expect a hardworking GP to be, had already found a corner table.

"Hello, hello!" said Denise, standing up and opening her arms for a hug from each of them. "Don't think I've seen either of you since Briony and Ross's wedding."

"A memorable affair," said Izzy.

"How's things? All go in the cotton and thread trade?"

"More eventful than you'd imagine," said Penny.

Denise had already ordered a glass of house white. The waiter came to the table to take their order. Izzy felt it rude to let Denise drink alone and ordered a wine spritzer. Penny went for a more restrained soda and lime. Main courses of prawns, mussels and roasted vegetables and goats cheese were ordered, and the waiter retreated to the kitchen counter.

"I like the food here," said Denise. "Across the county a lot of places just seem to serve nothing but 'n' chips."

"Un-chips?" said Penny.

"You   know.   Fish'n'chips.   Sausage'n'chips. Chicken'n'chips."

"'n' chips dishes would make my boyfriend very happy," said Izzy.

"Oh, yes," said Denise. "Did I hear you'd moved in with the dog whisperer?"

"And discovered his worrying fondness for potatoes," said Penny.

Izzy snapped a breadstick. "Right, we're going to play a game, and it's called Rate my Potato dish."

"Er, sure," said Denise.

"Rate my tater," said Penny. "Sounds fun."

"I will describe a potato dish and you will give it a

number of stars," said Izzy. "I'm looking for the hands-down winners in the potato game."

"Whoa, whoa, whoa," Penny said. "You can't just expect me to give it a single rating."

"What? Why not? That's exactly what I need."

"No, it can't be like that. I think you're looking for a rating that says whether it's a crowd-pleaser, but there are other dimensions. What about how healthy it is? What about whether it goes with loads of different dishes?"

"Fine," Izzy rolled her eyes. "Do the healthy one; but I am mainly looking for the crowd pleaser thing. Something that would knock the socks off a potato fan."

"A certain Polish potato fan. Understood," said Denise.

"I will start with boiled potatoes," said Izzy.

"Are they new potatoes? That makes a difference."

Izzy hummed. "Yes, let's say they are boiled new potatoes."

"Yum," said Denise.

"Are they Jersey Mids?" said Penny. "Because those are—"

"Can I have a number of stars please?" Izzy needed to be firm, she could see that.

"Four," said Denise.

"Five if they are Jersey Mids," said Penny.

"They get a five for being healthy too," added Denise. "Assuming we are boiling them in their skins. Are we?"

"Moving on," said Izzy. "Next up we have roast potatoes."

"Nice," said Penny. "A five for being yummy."

"A two for being a bit unhealthy," said Denise.

"Sauté potatoes," said Izzy.

"Same as roast," said Penny, with a dismissive wave of her hand.

"So swift to lump all potatoes together," said Denise.

They gently argued back and forth until the waiter returned with three wide-brimmed bowls of fragrant food. Monty grumbled under the table but stayed still.

Denise's mussels steamed enticingly. "You said you wanted to pick my brains," she said.

"That's right," said Penny.

"Now, as Izzy knows, I get asked too many times, in the most inappropriate situations, to look at a person's unusual rash. I hope you've got something more interesting for me."

"Foxglove poisoning," said Penny simply.

"Ooh, okay. Digitalis. I take it you've not just consumed some because um, I'm afraid you'd probably not have long to live."

"We know someone who died of foxglove poisoning."

"I'm sorry to hear that."

"Know *of*," Izzy added. "No one personal to us. She drank it dried in tea. The seeds in fact."

"Oh dear."

"I wanted to know how long it would have taken to kill her," said Penny.

Denise hummed in thought. "From ingestion to death could be a few hours. It very much depends on the dosage. Dried foxglove would have more potency."

Penny stabbed her fork into a salad leaf. "Here's the thing – and it's an odd thing—"

"Okay."

"It seems the victim drank the foxglove then managed to write something down before dying."

"That's possible."

"A crossword," said Izzy.

"Excuse me?"

"My cousin is of the opinion that Sybil Catchpole drank the poison, realised she had been poisoned, then compiled a crossword with clues indicating she had been poisoned. Oh – and posted it before dying."

"I'm not saying that *is* what happened," said Penny. Seeing the disbelieving looks on Izzy and Denise's face she huffed. "But *could* that happen?"

"This is a real thing?" asked Denise. "Like not a story off telly? I don't get much chance to watch Netflix when I get home. It's like work, home, food, crash into bed."

"It's a real thing," said Penny.

Denise nodded, thought for a while, then shook her head. "Your real problem is whether the woman – Sybil, you say? – knew she had been poisoned. I don't know what foxglove tastes like. I hope never to find out. If she hadn't realised immediately then she wouldn't know something was wrong until the symptoms started. That's heart palpitations, drowsiness, probably nausea too. The number of older people who don't realise they're having a heart attack and just think they're having a 'funny turn'…"

"So, it's unlikely."

"Digitalis is used to make digoxin, which is a very useful drug for treating heart conditions. Consumed in quantities it will cause powerful heart contractions and arrhythmia: a fatal heart attack. In the grand scheme of things, not the worse way to go."

As Izzy chewed on cubes of goat cheese and strips of roasted peppers, she pondered on how GPs probably got to meet many people near the ends of their lives, and that there could be such things as good and bad deaths.

"Your individual did not drink poison then write a crossword, let alone have time to pop it in a post box," said Denise. "Sorry."

"Fair enough," said Penny, sounding a little put out.

"By the way," said Denise, "this is a much better quality of medical conversation than I was expecting."

"One final medical question," said Penny, getting out her phone to read the word on the screen. "Imatinib."

"Imatinib," said Denise. "Uh-huh. I know it."

"The woman, Sybil, had a prescription for it. I googled it. It's a cancer drug, right?"

"Dr Google is correct," Denise smiled.

"Can you tell me anything more than that?"

"It's quite a specific cancer drug. Do you know what cancer the patient had?"

"I wondered if you could help."

"That drug is used for several forms of cancer, but is most commonly prescribed for chronic myelogenous leukaemia."

"That's bad," said Izzy.

Maybe it was the way she said it, but it drew a laugh from Denise. "Yes. Cancer is bad. CML attacks white blood cells. From the name Sybil I take it this lady was an older woman."

Penny nodded.

"Imatinib is not a cancer-curing drug – it slows the

progress of the disease. Cancer can be much slower in older people anyway. One of the few advantages of being old. Without further information, I would hazard a guess that the cancer would have killed her eventually. Before she drank foxglove tea, I mean."

The three of them stared at nothing, taken by thoughts of deaths good and bad.

"Hasselback potatoes," said Izzy.

"Pardon?" said Denise.

"Rate my potato. Hasselbacks."

"What are those?" asked Penny.

"You make them like roasts, but you slice them into thin wedges that are left joined at the bottom. Makes them more crispy."

"Oh ho! Someone found a way to make roast potatoes less healthy," said Denise.

"But probably very tasty," said Penny. "Five stars."

"You do know you've given everything five stars so far?" said Izzy.

"Oh. Yes, I can see how that might be a problem. I just really want to eat some potatoes now. Ask me about mashed potato, I would only give that a four."

"Thank you. Valuable research."

Denise raised her glass to toast her tablemates, saw her glass was empty, and signalled the waiter for a refill.

21

F riday morning breakfast was a stress-free meal at Marcin's place, probably because it didn't have any potato components. Both Izzy and Marcin ate cereal, and liked the occasional treat of pancakes, or even a full English breakfast. They crunched Coco Pops in companiable silence, then Marcin washed the dogs' bowls to feed them too.

"Oh hey, I might be a little busy this evening," he said. "I have some friends coming over to help me with something."

"Oh nice, will they stay for a meal?" Izzy asked.

"No. It's not that sort of thing. We will be out in the grounds, so you might not see us at all."

Izzy thought as she sipped her tea. Marcin's place was spacious, but it didn't extend to hundreds of acres. They surely wouldn't be more than two hundred yards from the house.

"Righto," she said slowly.

AT WORK in Cozy Craft that morning, Izzy was given strict instructions not to stray outside the area protected by plastic sheeting while she used messy dye for the kaftan project. It was a large enough area, including half of a cutting table and a large portion of the floor, but she still felt the siren call of the area just beyond the plastic. She recognised it as the basic human need to test boundaries. Wherever there was a button clearly marked Do Not Push, there would be an inevitable queue of people waiting in line to slam a decisive fist straight down on it.

She had the tied-up kaftans in a neat line, and she had mixed up the dye in lidded containers, one for each colour. She opened the blue one and dipped a paintbrush into the liquid. It was very runny. Maybe the plastic had been a good idea. She held the brush over the container to catch the worst of the drips and painted the rolled-up garment. At this point, the only decision to make was how much dye to use. A good balance was essential. It would be a dull kaftan if there were huge expanses of white, so she went over it several times, sploshing lots of liquid into the crevices.

Monty stood close by, interested, but not interested enough to risk getting splashed. In many ways, he was a timid dog.

"We also have some memory bears to finish today," Penny reminded Izzy. "And I had an idea of how we could make them even more fun."

"I'm all in favour of fun."

"You've spent all of Lent limiting yourself to one project at a time, you must have a lot of pent up 'fun' inside you."

"You have no idea. I'm still annoyed with myself that I didn't put a in bid for those fleeces that were for sale."

"I've been thinking about the crossword thing," said Penny. "We should talk to Gwen and Barry again."

"Yeah? What for?"

"They might not know about the crossword clues. We could explain to them and see if it prompts any thoughts. They might even know who Sybil hoped to alert with her clues."

"Do you think we should rake up the past and cause them that pain?"

"The man's a metal detector. Digging up the past and finding answers is clearly part of his nature."

"I think they're called detectorists."

Penny frowned. "You can't just make up words and claim they're real." She hummed thoughtfully. "Funny how Barry and Sybil are similar like that."

"Like how?"

"Well, metal detecting and crossword setting are not a million miles apart, are they? Sybil's treasure-hunting book and all that. Clues and wotnot."

Izzy frowned as she mentally compared the two quite different hobbies. "They aren't that similar really, are they?"

"They are both a bit esoteric and geeky, don't you think?" Penny said.

Izzy made a grunt of agreement, mainly to cover up the fact she was hastily mopping up a small spill of blue dye from the uncovered part of the cutting mat. How on earth had she splashed it beyond the plasticky boundary?

"We could go along to the metal detecting club tonight and ask him there," said Penny.

"Good idea! They probably have theories about the golden bell too."

"Oh. Good point."

Izzy opened another of the containers and grabbed a fresh brush to apply red dye to the next kaftan. It was mesmerising to apply the crimson dye to the pale fabric and watch the colour spread. She risked a little flicking of the dye onto the fabric.

"The victim was stabbed by a taller person, the direction of the blood spatter proves it," she intoned in a sinister voice.

"What are you doing?" Penny called.

"I'm using the red dye. I think I'm legally obliged to pretend I'm analysing a crime scene," said Izzy.

"Just as long as the shop doesn't look like one after you've finished. How long before we can open the kaftans out and see how they look?" asked Penny.

"If we open them too soon, the dye might run where we don't want it. We need to be patient."

Izzy heard her own words, recognising she wasn't by nature a patient woman. She could force herself to wait, but that wasn't the same. A really patient person was someone who set a crossword to announce the method of their own death. Izzy found it odd – and more than a little frightening – that someone might do such a thing.

Izzy put the wet items to one side. "That'll do for now."

"Now, the memory bears," said Penny. "My thought was this. You mentioned using Sybil's costume jewellery. Some was pinned to her wall, and I think I saw some boxes too. Why don't we go over to the cottage tomorrow and find each bear some sort of suitable adornment? For instance, an easy win would be a little butterfly brooch for Houseplant Jungle bear."

Izzy collected the bears and lined them all up on the counter so she and Penny could look at them. "I think we did a great job on these. You're right though: some bling would really enhance that whole 'more is more' aesthetic Sybil had. Peacock bear is easy. We find something with large colourful stones in the right colours. "What about Autumn Leaf bear?"

Penny waved a hand. "I can't be totally sure, as I get a kind of sensory overload every time I go to Avalon Cottage, but I reckon I saw one of those metal brooches that's made from a real leaf."

Izzy looked sceptical. "What? A real leaf? How does that work?"

"You get a leaf and, um—" Penny faltered. "I have no idea. But I know you can get them."

"Fine. Moroccan Souk bear should be easy. I bet she had some lovely trinkets from the time they spent there. I'll find a bag and we can take the bears over with us to have a mooch."

"No need," said Penny, waving her notebook. "Don't forget about the palettes I created in here. We can use those for reference." She sounded as if she was trying to keep the smugness from her voice, but not succeeding very well.

"Oh, and if we go over to Avalon Cottage," Izzy said, "it would be a fine opportunity to put back all those things you 'borrowed' while looking for clues, hmmm? The newspapers, the books, et cetera..."

"Maybe," said Penny. "But tonight we go to metal detecting club, yes?"

Izzy pulled a face. "Penny, would you be all right to go to the metal detecting thing on your own?"

"Er, sure. Why?"

"I need to do something at Marcin's place."

The words felt odd coming out of Izzy's mouth, and she wondered if she sounded suspicious. But what could she say? That she wanted to be close to home so she could spy on Marcin? That she wanted to know why he was inviting people over but keeping her away from them? That he was making strange clanking noises in the barn with the brand-new lock on the door?

"Yeah, I just need to do something," she said.

22

In Penny's mind, both she and Izzy would go to the metal detecting club. Each of them might hang around with someone different and see what they could learn. But Penny had agreed to go solo. Izzy and Marcin were very new to the whole business of sharing their space with each other, and Penny thought Izzy was over-compensating slightly. She probably had plans to knit potato cushions or something.

After a swift dinner and a walk for little Monty, Penny headed out and walked the short distance up Church Street to the Castle Community Rooms: a modern, single-storey village hall-type structure set back among the trees by the castle.

There were lights on inside. With only a moment's hesitation at stepping into a new place, she went inside to find just short of a dozen people setting out chairs in a loose circle and chatting to one another. A stout woman in a tweed jacket raised her hand in greeting. Once it was established that Penny had meant to come here and wasn't in the wrong place (a common occurrence apparently) she was made to feel very welcome. She was offered a cup of tea, and several people approached her to chat about their hobby.

Penny soon learned two things. First, the people who used metal detectors as a hobby were indeed called detectorists—

"Our Colin is trying to popularise the term 'dirt fishers'," said the tweedy woman with a smile.

"When people ask me what I am," said an older man with the beginnings of a Santa Claus beard. "I just say I'm an optimist, don't I, Leslie?"

"You need to be," agreed the woman, Leslie.

The second thing Penny learned – and it seemed very obvious now she thought about it – was that no actual detecting took place at the meeting. It was more of a check-in so that members could compare notes and discuss where they had been operating. It was probably a rather solitary hobby, like gardening or writing or photography, and maybe such hobbyists needed to get together once in a while to re-affirm social links with one another.

AFTER DINNER IZZY left the farm, telling Marcin she was meeting Penny to attend the metal detecting club. In her mind she justified this by telling herself she might go along later. Her mind recognised the lie and chastised her, but Izzy was burning with curiosity. She doubled back and shut herself into the tiny outbuilding which held the washing machine and tumble drier. The only other thing in there was an outside toilet in a small side room. The toilet was so old-fashioned it still featured a pull-chain flush. It was highly unlikely that Marcin would come in here and discover her hiding place. A rusty deckchair hung on the back of the door, so she was able to make herself comfortable while she watched the yard.

She saw several vehicles arrive, and people got out. Marcin came and greeted them all, then led them away in the direction of the forbidden barn. One of them had been Aubrey, painter and decorator, and Penny's one-time-not-quite-boyfriend.

Izzy texted Penny.

Marcin's being weird and secretive about something. He has a secret men-only club in his barn. Aubrey is there!

Penny texted back.

Did you stay home to spy on your boyfriend??

Izzy tried to think of a reply that didn't make her sound like a monster.

PENNY PUT her phone away and saw Barry Catchpole at a side table, digging through a pile of reference books that someone had placed there. When he saw her looking his way he nodded in recognition and came over.

"You're one of the house clearance women, aren't you?" he said.

"We met at your mum's place, yes. We've been commissioned by Gwen to make memory bears."

"Memory bears, yes."

"You found a useful book then?" she asked, with a nod to the paperback in his hand.

"*Spinks* is a great reference, even if this one's a little out of date," he said, tapping the book, which was about coins. "So you're interested in joining the club?"

"I am definitely interested in understanding a bit more about it," said Penny honestly. "It must be very relaxing."

He laughed. "Well, we tell ourselves that it's relaxing, but it's like any other hobby. It has its ups and downs. It even has its own politics and pecking order."

"How is that possible? Surely you all have the same sort of aims?"

"Good grief, no!" He caught sight of someone. "Geoffrey! Over here!" The older man with the nascent Santa beard wandered over from the table of tea and biscuits. "Geoff, this young lady thinks that all detectorists have the same aims. What would you say to that?"

Geoffrey gave a sad smile and clicked his teeth, as though he was about to run through the reasons why Penny's car was going to fail its MOT. "No, no, no. You'll never get that. It's the basic human condition in a nutshell, believe it or not. There's people who do it for the love of the thing. The thrill of tracking something down. They do as much work looking at books and maps and whatnot as they do on the ground. Then there's the social members, like Davey there." He gestured with a thumb to another member. "They come here for the tea and the company."

"And biscuits," said Davey, overhearing.

"That's fair enough," said Geoffrey. "Then there's other types. Glory hunters, but in different ways. Some like to have the latest equipment. Always trying to get one up in whatever way they can with their fancy expensive doodahs. Glen there has just bought an XP Deus for just shy of eight hundred quid. Dun't need it, but he likes having it. Going to give it a test run when we meet up next Tuesday at Aldham Farm, which you should definitely come to. And of course there's the treasure hunters."

"Treasure hunters?"

Geoffrey grinned. "Oh, look at her eyes light up! Oh aye, there are some people who think they're going to find the next Staffordshire Hoard. There's plenty of them who'll stop at nothing to get something valuable."

"Which sort are you?" asked Penny.

Barry and Geoffrey exchanged a glance and Penny could see an obvious warmth between the men.

"Well, I can't afford to be the one with the latest equipment," said Geoffrey with a smile. "I think we both do it to exercise ourselves in every sense. It can be a workout for the brain and the body. It's a form of meditation."

"I was fascinated to hear the story about your mother's book," Penny said to Barry. "I can imagine that a golden bell would be a very satisfying thing to find."

Barry's face hardened. "That thing can stay in the ground for eternity for all I care. It's for attention seekers and fools. Brings out the worst of the treasure hunters."

Geoffrey tilted his head. "On the other hand, it has brought people into our world over the years. It's the initial lure which draws them in. Some of those have turned out to be all right."

"Is it just the treasure hunters, though?" Penny asked.

"Hmmm?"

"*The Golden Bell.* I recently picked up a copy of the book. It seems as though it's designed for armchair detectives. I bet people have turned up here like I have tonight with theories to share?"

"Course they have!" said Barry with a laugh. "Theories are ten a penny, but none of them ever come to anything. Sometimes, I don't think my mother ever hid the bell. It would have been found by now, wouldn't it?"

Penny gave a shrug. "England's a big place." She glanced at Barry. "Can I ask you, has anyone spoken to you about the crosswords your mother created for the local paper?"

"Crosswords? No." Barry stared at her. "I mean, it sounds as if it could be her sort of thing. It's very much her sort of thing."

Penny nodded. "She submitted them under a pseudonym. The last one she did is quite surprising. Look at the answers." She had the page from the *Frambeat Gazette* in her bag. She brought it out and unfolded it for him.

He glanced down at the list of words and a frown knitted across his face. "What?"

"The clues. Poison, foxglove, Sybil."

"That's just... That's just weird. A coincidence, surely?"

"I really don't have any idea," said Penny. "That's part of the reason for sharing it."

"Let's have a look," said Geoffrey.

"You've told other people?" said Barry. "What did they make of it?"

"Nothing much," said Penny.

"Probably nothing then," said Barry, balling the sheet up in his fist. He dropped the screwed-up paper into Penny's hand and walked away to join the group of people sitting down for the formal part of the meeting.

She texted Izzy, curious about what her daft cousin was up to.

The club is going to be finished in an hour or so. Want me to come over?

IN THE DARK on her little deckchair, Izzy read Penny's text. She would have enjoyed having a partner in crime, but she didn't want this to get out of hand. It was already a bit out of hand.

No. Let's talk tomorrow. Unless you want to text Aubrey and ask him what he's doing?

Penny's reply was prompt.

I am DEFINITELY not doing that. Talk tomorrow. Oh, and you're coming metal detecting on Tuesday.

Izzy folded the deckchair and hung it back on the door. She should go back inside and start acting like a normal person—

She heard the sound of footsteps and voices outside.

"Toilet is in there, past the washing machine and round the corner," said Marcin.

Izzy froze. She had half a second in which she could

reveal herself and maybe say she was doing laundry. Except there was no laundry. She wished she had thought to bring the kaftans out with her so she could at least unfurl and wash them; but they were sitting in the shop inside a carrier bag. She slipped behind the door and squeezed into the gap as the door swung open. She saw Aubrey walk past her and turn into the side room containing the toilet. She tried hard to turn off her ears and not listen, but it was impossible. The toilet flushed with a loud clanking sound, and Aubrey walked back through. There was a moment where he could easily have seen Izzy in her lousy hiding place, but his eyes were seeking out something else. He found the sink next to the washing machine and washed his hands. At this point he was on the other side of the door, so unless he pulled it shut, Izzy was safe from discovery. She realised with horror that the towel was hanging on the back of the door. She unhooked it and pushed it out to the side. If Aubrey wondered what it was hanging on he didn't bother checking. He quickly dried his hands and walked out into the courtyard, where the others were gathered.

"I had a lot of fun. Same time tomorrow?" Aubrey said.

"If you don't mind," came Marcin's voice.

There was the slamming of car doors and the sound of the vehicles driving away. Now Izzy just needed to escape from the outhouse and make her way back inside without looking suspicious.

23

P enny raised an eyebrow as Izzy entered the shop the following day. Monty lifted his head from his basket too. "So, why were you spying on Marcin?" Penny asked. "Tell me all about it."

"Am I am being a crazy stalker girlfriend?" said Izzy.

Penny shrugged. "I don't know. Go fetch us a bacon roll for breakfast and Dr Penny will analyse your mind."

And so they sat and drank their morning tea with hot bacon rolls while Izzy described Marcin's puzzling behaviour.

"Yep, it's a weird one," said Penny. "Have you tried asking Marcin?"

"Confront him?"

"I said ask him. But sure, confront him."

Izzy dabbed a spot of ketchup from the corner of her mouth. "When I think of confrontation, I think of complaining about something that is obviously wrong and villainous. If I confront him with this I am just going to look like a paranoid idiot. He hasn't done anything bad, as far as I know. I mean, I can't imagine Aubrey turning up to watch an illegal bareknuckle boxing match, can you?"

"He's running illegal boxing matches?"

"No. I'm saying I don't think he's running illegal boxing matches. Or anything like that. I just don't know *what* he's doing. It's probably completely fine. I just feel hurt that I'm being shut out from whatever it is."

Penny sighed. "I see that. Listen, don't fret. Just try and put it from your mind."

"Yeah. I suppose. Anyway, I want to hear about your club visit last night."

"Ha! It was really quite nice. A bit geeky, I suppose."

"We would sound horribly geeky to anyone who listened to us talk about sewing," Izzy pointed out.

"True, true. I mean, it was all rather niche. People brought together by a very specific hobby. But they're enthusiastic. We've been invited to go metal detecting on Tuesday with them."

"Okay. Was Barry there?"

"He was."

"You told him about the crossword? I bet that stopped him being so grumpy."

"No," sighed Penny. "I think he's just a grumpy person. He had a friend with him, an older guy. They were polite enough, but Barry screwed up the crossword." Penny showed Izzy the flattened-out mess.

"Well that is just rude," said Izzy.

"Of course," said Penny in a light and meaningful tone,

"Barry might have good reason to want the whole crossword thing die a death."

"You still think he put the foxglove in his mum's tea?"

"I don't think it. I'm just putting it out there as a theory. Laying one's hands on an inheritance can be a strong motivator, especially if he's got money problems and estranged from his mum."

"Has he got money problems?"

"Again, it's just a theory. Who else would have reason to kill her?"

"What about Gwen?"

"Gwen?" said Penny, surprised. "The loving daughter? The one who commissioned the memory bears?"

"That could be the actions of a guilty conscience. But I'm thinking in terms of a mercy killing."

"Because Sybil had cancer?"

"A slow death. Foxglove poisoning would have been quicker and, relatively speaking, less painful."

Penny looked unsure. "Mercy killing for your mum without her consent? That's cold."

Izzy sighed and sipped her tea. "Then maybe we're missing the obvious. It wasn't murder or an accident. It was self-inflicted. Sybil was dying and didn't want it drawn out, so—"

"She wrote the crossword as a suicide note, then drank tea she had poisoned herself."

Izzy considered the possibility. "It would certainly explain how such a keen gardener could do something as daft as poison herself by accident. Maybe it is as simple as that." Finished with her roll, Izzy folded the paper bag it had come in and which she had been using as a plate. "Right, I'm going to rinse the dye off the kaftans."

"Will they need to go through a full wash?" asked Penny.

"Yeah, but I thought I might undo them and rinse them here so you can see the big reveal," Izzy grinned. She disappeared up to the kitchen with the bag holding the soggy kaftans. It took quite a lot of rinses before Izzy called down to Penny.

"There was a small flaw in my plan. I rinsed them all until the excess dye was gone, but now I have soggy fabric. I can't walk round the shop with it or I'll drip water everywhere. Come up and see the pretty patterns!"

Penny laughed at Izzy's attempts to hold the dripping garments over the draining board. "They look amazing!" The patterns stood out beautifully. Izzy had done two of the kaftans in horizontal stripes and two in concentric circles. "The balance between the white and the colour is just perfect. I can't wait to see them when they are dry and ironed. How on earth are you going to carry them home?"

"I'll put them in a bag and stick them straight into the wash when I get back. In the meantime they can sit on the draining board."

In the afternoon, with the sun shining on their faces, Izzy and Penny walked to the edge of town and up the lane to Avalon Cottage. Izzy carried a heavy woven shopping bag which contained the newspapers, notepad, and coded journal they had borrowed on their last somewhat frantic visit. Izzy had taken photos of the first dozen pages of the journal and said she was going to ask her colleagues at the *Frambeat Gazette* to help her decode it.

They let themselves in with Gwen's key once more, and as Penny went about the task of putting all items back in place, Izzy began a casual search for accoutrement and accessories which they could use to personalise the memory bears.

Penny re-joined Izzy up in the bedroom and immediately pointed to something on the dressing table. "Here we are. A metal leaf."

Izzy leaned over to see.

There was a velvet stand at the rear of the dressing table. Both sides were padded so that brooches could be stuck into it for display. Penny pointed at the bronze-coloured leaf near to the top.

"Huh." Izzy plucked it off the stand. "A leaf skeleton. Do you think the original leaf is inside, or was this made by peeling the leaf away and leaving the impression?"

Penny shrugged. "I spy some nice peacock-coloured stones on there too. Now I'm looking out for a butterfly."

Izzy gazed across at a chest of drawers. "Would a dragonfly work?"

Penny looked where Izzy pointed. The dragonfly was mounted on a pedestal mirror using Blu-tack. "Oh, that's lovely. Yes, it would."

They were carefully collecting up treasures for each of the bears when there was a knock at the door. It took Izzy a moment to realise it was coming from the back door, not the front. They looked at each and silently went to go see who it was.

Alison Atkinson from next door waved through the

kitchen window. She seemed to deflate somewhat when she saw it was them.

Penny opened the door. "Good afternoon."

"Good afternoon." A smile rearranged the wrinkles on her tanned face. "Moved in, have we?"

Penny laughed dutifully. "Just back to collect some trinkets for decorating the memory bears." She held up a couple as evidence.

"Ah, yes," said Alison. "And don't forget those tie-dye garments for us to wear at the wake on Wednesday. I hope they look good."

"We shall see," said Izzy. "They've yet to dry, so..."

Alison made to look past them as though expecting someone else. "I was hoping to see Gwen."

"Not with us, I'm afraid."

"Blast. I really did want a word. It's— Am I being unreasonable?"

"Unreasonable?" said Penny.

"Come see, come see." Alison beckoned them out into the garden.

Izzy noticed that below the rather lively dungarees Alison was wearing, she had nothing on her bare feet. Clearly the old hippie sensibilities died hard, Izzy thought.

The garden seemed to have blossomed more since Penny and Izzy were last there. Bluebells and forget-me-nots cast a sprinkle of vivid blues. Blossoming primula countered that with a scattering of yellow, and Izzy saw some colourful fritillaries starting to show. There was no buzz of pollinating bees, but looking at this riot of colour she didn't imagine it would be long before they were out in force, busying from plant to plant.

"It's causing terrible problems with our foundations," said Alison.

She led them past the fence panel/gate and to the tree at the bottom of the garden. "Everyone knows you shouldn't plant ash trees within fifty feet of buildings," she said.

"Is that so?" said Izzy, who didn't know but was always keen to learn new things.

"The roots go off in all directions in search of water," said the older woman, imitating questing roots with her own bent fingers.

"Bane of our lives," said her husband, Horace, from the gap in the fence.

Izzy gave him a cheery wave. He smiled toothily. "No Gwen?" he said.

"Sadly not," said Alison.

His playful expression shifted from Alison to the visitors. "Care for a cup of cha then?" he said.

24

In the Atkinson's garden, a gazebo mostly composed of wicker and natural wood had been erected. On its elevated platform Horace poured herbal fruit teas and served moist slices of vegan carrot cake.

"This looks lovely," said Penny.

Izzy gazed round at the garden, which was no less lavish than Sybil's, although the house at the far end was considerably larger and grander.

Horace saw her looking. "I know, I know. Sybil and Ivor were happy to live in modest digs, even when raising two children, but I could not resist the lure of consumerism."

"Pish," said Alison, smiling. "You both inherited these properties from your parents. It was only by chance that your parents' house was far grander." She turned to Penny and Izzy. "He sometimes likes to play up to the notion of solicitors as soulless and greedy."

"I believe the cliché is that solicitors are stuffy and dull more than greedy," he countered.

"You were always Sybil's solicitor?" said Penny.

"Until recently," he said. "Throughout Ivor's life certainly, until—" He waved his hand rather vaguely towards Sybil's garden. "We get cantankerous as we get older."

"Stuck in our ways," nodded Alison.

"Harder to love," Horace concluded, smacking his gums together for solemn emphasis.

"Sybil had been ill for a while, hadn't she?" said Penny.

Alison, holding her tea in both hands like a bowl, nodded. "It was debilitating. The tiredness. The joint pains she used to get. Forced her to give up painting about, hmmm, maybe a year ago."

"That's sad," said Izzy.

"That's when the life went from her," Horace agreed. "She was always ambitious. Aggressively so."

"I would say so," said Alison. "She liked fame. No – she liked the recognition."

"That brief spell of fame in the seventies and eighties. Gave her a taste."

"If any of us was a greedy capitalist, it was probably our Sybil."

"God rest her soul," said Horace.

"Yes," said Alison.

"In fact, we had been out celebrating the success of her book on the night of the crash."

"*That* crash?" said Izzy.

"Yes, that crash," said Horace. "Poor man. Very sad. We'd been up to the pub in Yoxford. Oh, we'd all been drinking that night, but Ivor had put away enough whisky to anaesthetise a buffalo."

"Horace!" said Alison.

"Well, it's true, dear. Surprising he could walk straight, let alone drive. But attitudes were somewhat different back then."

"Really?" said Penny.

Horace gave it a cautious nod. "Indeed. Drink driving was the preserve of the cheeky scamp; the person who knew they shouldn't but did anyway. They weren't held in the same contempt as they are now. Well, even I was probably over the limit when I drove home that night. There but for the grace of God..."

Alison shook her head. "The scandal hit her career. Follow-up books were not a success at all. She might as well have mown that poor chap down herself."

The tea was indeed fruity, but there was also a strong herbal flavour to it; the kind of flavour one might associate with the phrase 'Drink it up, it's good for you.' Izzy gazed at the flecks of leaves resting at the bottom of the reddish-brown drink.

"Do you mind if I ask about Sybil's death?" she said.

"Ask away," said Horace. "Can't think there's anything that we've not discussed or asked ourselves in the months since."

"It occurred to us that it seems unlikely she would poison herself with foxglove by accident."

"Yes?"

"And we had wondered—"

"Not that we've been idly chit-chatting about the dead,"

said Penny quickly, even though that was exactly what they had been doing.

"No," said Izzy. "But it had occurred to us that Sybil, knowing she was gravely ill and only going to get worse... Well, we'd wondered if she'd killed herself. Deliberately, I mean."

Horace smiled, which struck Izzy as an odd response to such a macabre topic. Then she realised it was a smile of indulgence; of patience.

"This was raised and discussed for quite some time at the coroner's inquest," he said. "Seems plausible, doesn't it?"

"The problem is the jars," said Alison. "The jars in the kitchen."

Izzy recalled the shelves lined with matching glass jars: all empty and clean.

"She kept her various tea blends in the jars in the kitchen. All her herbs and spices, and goodness knows what."

"You'd think she was into witchcraft, the amount she had," said Horace. "Probably was."

"Thing is, the foxglove seeds which killed her were thoroughly mixed in with one of her own tea blends. Thoroughly."

"Does that mean she didn't kill herself?" Penny asked.

Izzy understood. "If she had meant to end her own life, she'd have just put the deadly seeds in her pot, or cup, or whatever."

"Give herself a full-strength dose," said Horace. "But if she had knowingly put them in the jar, mixed them in— First of all, how would she know if she was giving herself a fatal dose? And, more importantly, would she leave the poisoned jar if there was even the smallest possibility of a family member or visitor later taking a cup for themselves?"

"She was self-centred and driven and increasingly bitter in her old age," said Alison. "But she was not wantonly cruel."

"So, it had to be—" Izzy stopped herself because she was about to say, 'had to be someone else who put the seeds there', but mentally swerved at the last moment and managed to say, "—had to be an accident."

"For certain," said Horace. "Life is full of strange and cruel twists." He reached out and placed his hand over his wife's and squeezed lovingly.

Penny took a deep breath, as though trying to inhale all the beauty of the Atkinson's garden. "It is lovely out here. Do you know if Gwen or Barry might want to move in next door? Assume they are due to inherit."

"Nothing to inherit," said Horace. "One of the last things I did for Sybil before ... before she became difficult, was to arrange for the house to be signed over to the children. Sybil wanted to avoid the messiness of inheritance and any tax issues by making a gift of the house to her children."

"So, it was already theirs," said Izzy and recalled how Barry had said as much when they'd met him in the cottage.

THAT EVENING, Izzy walked home with the still wet kaftans in a broad tub. She went into the outhouse to load the garments straight into the washing machine. While putting them in she heard voices outside. It sounded like Aubrey and Marcin. She immediately froze and cocked an ear, even though it felt foolish and embarrassing to be eavesdropping in what she had already started to think of as her new home.

"Hell of a thing you've done there," came Aubrey's voice.

Izzy strained to hear Marcin's reply, but she heard nothing but a vague rumble that might have been agreement or regret.

They disappeared into the house and shut the door.

Izzy finished loading the washing machine and went inside into the kitchen.

"Hi Izzy," said Aubrey, waggling the mug that Marcin was about to top up from the teapot.

"Tea?" Marcin asked.

"Yes please. What have you been up to?" Izzy asked.

Marcin and Aubrey exchanged a look and both smiled. Izzy felt her face fall into an expression of dismay. They weren't even bothering to hide that they were up to something.

"Aubrey is helping me with something," said Marcin. "I fear I may be trying his patience."

"Not at all, mate. Not at all," said Aubrey with a wide smile. He drained his mug. "I'd better be going. See you next time, eh?"

Izzy was fuming at the sly exchange between Marcin and Aubrey. She couldn't quite articulate why it was so annoying. She had suffered no actual harm – but she was clearly being excluded from something by her boyfriend. Was this another thing about relationships? Where her expectation wasn't matching up to other people's reality? Couples might want privacy for some part of their lives.

"Izzy," said Marcin.

"What?" she snapped, her thoughts – her angry thoughts – interrupted.

"I am sorry," he said. "I have startled you. Tea?"

"I have had enough tea today," she retorted.

He nodded. It was a small nod, a careful nod. "Can I ask you something?"

"I don't know. Can you?"

"I wonder if I perhaps must ask you to forgive me."

"Why? What have you done?"

He pressed his lips together. "My question: if a person does something foolish but does it for the very best of reasons, is it any less foolish?"

"Eh? Is this a test, or are you reading it from a fortune cookie?" Izzy asked.

Marcin sighed. "It is possible that I have bitten off more than I can chew. You might not be impressed with me."

"Are you running an illegal boxing match?"

"What?"

"Drug-dealing? A counterfeit jeans operation?"

"I – what? No. I ... I want you to be patient with me and please understand that I do this for love."

Izzy's eyebrows shot up. Marcin had mentioned the L word. He hadn't mentioned it as a big declaration, just as a simple matter of fact while he was mumbling vaguenesses. It made Izzy feel warm inside, but also slightly angry – because now she could no longer feel mad about his secretive meetings.

She looked at the confusion in his eyes, guessing she must have nothing but confusion in her own. There was tenderness there, but also worry. She flung her arms around him and hugged him. He hugged her back with equal fierceness.

25

Izzy had hung the kaftans on the racks in the outhouse, and on Monday morning she collected them on her way to work. When she arrived at Cozy Craft, Penny had already made drinks for them.

"I'm going upstairs to iron these kaftans," said Izzy.

"I can't wait to see how they've turned out," said Penny, following behind. Monty seemed less impressed with the prospect, and he snoozed on in his basket.

Izzy switched the iron on and pulled out the blue kaftan first, shaking it free of its largest creases. "This one is in horizontal stripes." She smoothed it with the iron and they both studied the finish.

"It's a lovely job, Izzy. The colour has made a subtle texturing on every single part of the fabric."

Izzy nodded. Not many parts of the fabric were solid white or solid blue. There was an interesting marbling which filled the gaps between the stripes. She ironed the entire garment, then slipped it over a wooden hanger that was hooked on the picture rail running around the walls. They could see how it hung as a garment, and it looked good.

"Red next!" Izzy unfurled the red one from the bag.

Penny grabbed the bottom and they flapped it loose like a bedsheet.

"Gorgeous!" Penny said. "It's very slightly different."

"I started in a different place when I gathered it up," said Izzy. "They are all roughly the same pattern, but this one I gathered in at the middle to make the long thin sausage shape, then tied it at intervals."

The orange and purple ones were equally successful. After ironing and hanging them all up, they stood back, sipping their tea to admire Izzy's work.

"It's an arresting sight," said Penny.

"Shame we can't put them in the window for a while," said Izzy.

"Gwen wants them as soon as possible," said Penny, "and it's only right they should debut at Sybil's wake. We'd burst that bubble if we put them up on display. It would feel a bit disrespectful."

"We could always make some more for a future window display," said Izzy. "I made a start on accessories."

Penny looked puzzled as Izzy rummaged inside a bag that was not yet empty.

"I wanted to make sure the dye didn't go to waste, so I used it up on some other bits and pieces." Izzy pulled the first thing out. "A tote bag!" She dived back in, like a conjuror searching for their next pigeon. "A pencil case and a hair scrunchie!"

"Did you just make a bunch of things out of cotton scraps?" asked Penny.

"Waste not, want not," said Izzy with a nod. "I'm not done. A cot sheet and a set of napkins."

"Is there a market for tie-dye cot sheets?" Penny asked.

"I think babies respond well to bright colours," said Izzy. "It could be very popular. And last but not least, I made a bone toy for Monty."

Izzy held it out proudly. The toy bone was tie-dyed with the red, looking as if it was fresh from the butcher's. Monty heard his name mentioned and trotted upstairs to see.

"Here you are Monty, enjoy!"

He savaged the bone briefly, putting on a show of appreciation, then retired to his basket to lie with his chin protectively across his new toy.

Penny spent some time adding the decorative jewellery to the bears and proudly lined them up for Gwen's inspection. A text from Gwen confirmed she'd be able to collect them after four. In preparation, Penny covered them up with a cloth, so that they could whip it off at the correct moment.

"Got to have some theatrics. This whole commission has been a bit theatrical," she said. Monty made a small noise. Was he looking for a bit part in this production? "Your job is to be the handsome background dog, Monty."

The customer arrived promptly at four.

"Hi Gwen. We have bears to show you." Penny indicated the covered row.

"Oh, you're like a magician! When do I get to see them?"

"It's just a small build-up," said Penny. "I wanted you to

see the notes first, so you can take a look at the fabrics we decided to use." She pushed the notebook towards Gwen.

Gwen ran her fingers across the front. "*Sybil's memory bears: project notes*. How thoughtful." She opened it up and gasped when she saw the neat rows of fabric samples. "Oh my, this is just lovely." She took a few minutes to absorb the details of each one. "You've left space for me to write when she might have worn some of these things." She stabbed a sample of red wool bouclé with a finger. "I remember her wearing this skirt a lot. She said the colour was perfect pillar box red."

"Oh yes!" said Izzy. "It really is." Izzy looked very excited as she pointed at the sheet, nodding to Penny to whisk it off and show the bears.

"We'll give Gwen a moment to look at the notebook. Tell us when you're ready to see the bears."

There were a few more long moments where Gwen paged through the book. Finally she looked up and smiled. "Show me!"

Penny removed the sheet and the bears were revealed.

"Oh my!" Gwen looked momentarily tearful. "I can't quite believe it. You have made bears that look so much like something mum would actually have bought. You captured her style so completely. I don't know what to say."

She looked away, overcome by powerful emotion. Penny gave her a moment.

"We're truly delighted you like them."

"Like them? I love them! They are perfect." Gwen opened up her arms and beckoned the two of them forward. She embraced them both. Izzy looked over at

Penny with a quizzical look on her face, slightly unsure of how to react.

Gwen released them and sighed deeply. "I know that grieving is a weird old process, but I feel as though the two of you have helped me somehow with this. I'm a little bit further along now you've made these gorgeous keepsakes. Thank you."

"And now the kaftans," said Izzy. They were still hanging in the workshop upstairs, so Izzy took Gwen up to see them.

Gwen gave a small exclamation of delight. "Exactly right. These are such fun!"

Izzy unhooked and folded them up so Gwen could take them away in a bag.

"I don't remember it at all, obviously," said Gwen. "But it must have been fun being a hippie. Peace and love, with a side helping of not having to wear a bra."

"Obviously you can do all of those things any time you want," said Izzy. "You don't need a label."

"True," said Gwen. "To be honest I don't really associate those things with my mother. I think she just liked the aesthetic."

They went downstairs where Penny rang up the sale.

"I don't suppose the two of you would like to come and lend some moral support when we wear these?" asked Gwen.

"At the funeral?" Penny asked.

Gwen nodded. "The wake is over in the community rooms."

"We could pop along, I'm sure."

Gwen jotted down the details for them and left with a smile.

Izzy turned to Penny. "I've never been to the funeral of a person I never met. What if someone asks me a question about how I knew Sybil?"

"It will be fine," said Penny firmly. "There won't be an exam."

26

Tuesday was a stitch and natter day, which was both pleasant and one of the easier days to manage in the shop.

Various locals – all women, despite Izzy's attempts to draw in some male stitchers – gathered on the first floor to work on their own personal projects in a friendly shared environment. All Penny and Izzy were required to do was provide them with hot drinks and biscuits, and occasionally keep the peace when a heated sewing-related argument broke out.

While Judith Conklin, the de facto head of the group (or at least its loudest member), held forth on the subject of American quilting methods, Izzy helped Sharon Burnley, who was just on the fiddly bit of the Easter bonnet she was making for her dog. Penny periodically whisked round with a big earthenware pot of tea and made sure the plate of hobnobs was well stocked.

The shop was otherwise quiet. Penny stood at the counter with Monty curled at her feet, and flicked through the pages of *The Golden Bell*. She had read through the story and admired the pictures and, yes, Annalise was right: the book didn't function particularly well as a children's story. The images, whilst charming, were somewhat disjointed, and there was no satisfying conclusion.

Penny read it again, intent on finding clues to the buried treasure. The first double-page spread seemed an ideal place to start. The book's hero, Sir Percival, was pictured riding through country lanes towards a castle on a hill that was very clearly modelled on Framlingham Castle. If Sybil based many of the book's features on the local area, it was no surprise treasure hunters might have thought the actual bell was buried close by.

In the picture, three local women in peasant's garb were holding up their hands beseechingly to Sir Percival as he rode by. One held an apple in her hand, another what looked like a little potted bonsai, and the third a slender white candle. They were odd items, the bonsai looking particularly anachronistic, and Penny wondered if they were significant clues.

Sir Percival wasn't looking at them at all, with his chin raised and an arm outstretched towards the castle. His finger pointed directly at the flag on the top of the castle, where a white flower stood against a red background.

"Clues, clues...," she muttered to herself, and pulled across a notepad to jot things down.

Penny didn't notice the passage of time until Izzy came down with a frown on her face.

"The ladies are demanding their cups be refilled. Are you perhaps too busy to assist?"

Penny looked up guiltily and glanced about, hoping the shop might be overrun with a sudden influx of wealthy customers. It was not.

"Sorry. I'll get right on it. Look—" she turned the book around "—Appletreewick."

"Pardon?" said Izzy.

Penny pointed out the three women in the picture and their gifts. "An apple, a tree, a candle or wick. Appletreewick."

"And that means something?"

"It's a village in Yorkshire. Wharfedale to be precise. I looked it up. It's a clue."

"I can see that's very thrilling," said Izzy, waggling the teapot in her hand.

"Yes, yes, of course." Penny took the pot and made more tea.

The stitch and natter group ended with smiles and progress from the stitching folk of Framlingham, and the rest of the morning in Cozy Craft passed both quietly and pleasantly. Having finished their recent commission, both of the women slipped into non-work tasks. Izzy had a bunch of 'Madame Zelda' horoscopes to write for this week's *Frambeat Gazette*, and Penny, using her laptop for research assistance, slipped further and further into the world of *The Golden Bell*.

There were, she discovered, a small number of chat groups and discussion pages about the search for the treasure. One featured various comments and threads which tackled the more obvious clues. Penny didn't know if it was cheating, or at least against the spirit of the book, to go through each page and see what clues the internet was willing to provide, but it was frankly irresistible.

She also slowly realised that nearly all the threads on this website had comments from two different users: *Monmouth Man* and *Jigsaw*. The comments stretched back to ones posted more than ten years ago, and continued almost up to the present day. *Monmouth Man*'s user icon was a medieval drawing of a monk, but *Jigsaw*'s was a photo of the man himself, or at least his eyes and forehead.

"It's Dougal Thumbskill," Penny said in recognition.

Both Izzy and Monty looked up at her exclamation. "Pardon?"

"On these treasure hunting forums. He's a real *Golden Bell* enthusiast."

"Which we sort of already knew."

"I really must go and pick his brains," said Penny, halfway to the door before she realised she intended to do so right now.

"You said we were going metal detecting this afternoon," said Izzy.

"I did. We will. I'll only be a minute."

Dougal's shop next to Cozy Craft was open that day. Penny went straight in.

The shop was closely packed with display shelves full of jigsaws, boardgames, and plastic kit models. There was a table where a wargaming battle between what appeared to be American GIs and Vietcong figurines took place in a muddy model landscape. Above the counter, model Spitfires and Lancaster bombers hung on threads from the ceiling. On a nearby shelf, a whole battalion of Napoleonic wargaming miniatures stood ready for battle, as though ready to take on the World War Two aircraft in a somewhat mismatched battle.

Dougal Thumbskill, proprietor, looked up and automatically put a smile upon his face at the approach of a customer. The smile faltered when he saw it was Penny. It vanished completely when he saw the book in her hand.

"Oh, found your own copy, have you?" he said. "And now come to pick my brains?"

"I just didn't realise you were such an enthusiast," she said.

"I consider myself an expert," he replied primly.

"I think I found a clue."

"Oh?"

"Appletreewick."

Dougal smiled thinly. "Page two. Yes. You're one of the Yorkists then?"

"Pardon?"

"Appletreewick. You'll also note that the flag on the castle is the banner of the House of York. If you move onto page eight, you will see elements that suggest Green, How and Hill. Greenhow Hill is also in the same area of Yorkshire."

"Oh. I see. That's interesting."

"I'm not a Yorkist," said Dougal. "It's a misdirect."

"So you're..."

"A Suffolkist, naturally. The bell is buried hereabouts. It's why I'm here."

It took Penny a moment to process what he was saying.

"You opened a shop in Fram just because you think the golden bell is buried here?"

His thin smile returned, although there was more humanity in this one. "I visited Suffolk many times for research and— I would not say I fell in love with Fram, but I could certainly see its charms. So when I decided to open a shop, ninety-seven that was, this seemed ideal." He clearly saw the surprise on Penny's face. "Oh, I'm not the only one to do that."

"You seem quite pally with this *Monmouth Man* on the chat forums," said Penny.

"Geoffrey? Ha! I wouldn't quite call it pally. A grudging respect between rivals, perhaps."

"Geoffrey?" She pointed in a general direction that might or might not have been towards the Community Rooms. "Metal detectorist Geoffrey?"

"Didn't you know? Absolutely passionate about finding the golden bell. Not the level of academic authority as me," said Dougal, straightening up a little as he said it. "And using crude detection equipment in his search. Of course, he's not had the advantages in life some of us have had, and when I was here he was—" Dougal halted in mid-sentence, cleared his throat, and tried to look composed. He seemed to be a man who, despite owning a shop, had little in the way of social graces. His attempts at naturalistic behaviour were clunky, to say the least.

"What is it?" said Penny.

"Let's just say he was residing at Her Majesty's Pleasure for the latter years of the twentieth century."

"He was in prison?"

"Nearly twenty years, I believe." Dougal held up his hands in a magnanimous gesture. "But I'm not one to hold that against a man. Let the past be the past. No need to dwell on it."

Penny made a doubtful noise. Despite Dougal's words, he clearly had very few reservations about sharing the sordid details of another man's past.

But twenty years in prison? Penny wondered what a man could have done to receive such a weighty sentence.

27

Penny and Izzy drove to the Suffolk Searchers club dig on Aldham Farm, just out of town. When they arrived at the field gate they met Davey, who was manning a table to welcome guests.

"Hallo! I'll need you to sign in and pop on a hi-vis please," he said, turning a clipboard around so they could add their details.

Penny could see people dotted around the field; most of them were not wearing hi-vis. Presumably they wanted to keep an eye on inexperienced guests.

"Thanks, Davey," she said as they handed back the clipboard. "Now, what do we do?"

"I will book out some detectors for you to use – basic ones you understand, not top of the line as some of us prefer. I will show you how to operate them. You can go and have a wander about, see what you find. If you want to investigate something by digging, I need you to raise a fist to the sky like this, then someone will come and talk you through the correct procedure for making a tidy hole. Once you've tried it a couple of times you'll get the hang of making it neat. We like to make our presence here *undetectable* to the landowner."

His elbows went out to the sides in a little waggle dance to emphasise his joke. Penny and Izzy smiled politely.

A few minutes later they were both practising on a bottle top fastened onto a piece of wood so they could demonstrate basic competence to Davey before they set off into the field.

They walked a few yards apart, swinging the detectors as they'd been shown.

"Got a good stance there," said Geoffrey.

Penny took off her detector headphones to speak to him. Seeing him now, in the light of her conversation with Dougal Thumbskill, it was very hard to imagine this genial older man as a convicted criminal. Sure, he had a bulk, a presence, but his manner was always soft; a teddy bear.

"Geoffrey, this is my cousin, Izzy," she said, gesturing.

"Pleased to meet you," Izzy said and shook his hand.

"Glad to see Penny is spreading the word about the attractions of the metal detecting hobby," he said.

"What's not to like? Getting out in the air, meeting people, maybe finding that fabled golden bell."

"Oh? Thinking of finding Catchpole's golden bell?"

"I'm sure we'd all like to find buried treasure," said Penny.

"Treasure, eh?" smiled Geoffrey. "We all want a piece of it, don't we? Trouble is, a lot of us don't realise when we have treasure right under our noses."

Izzy's nose wrinkled in confusion.

"You're talking about the sort of treasure that's not made of precious metals, aren't you?" Penny hazarded.

"Indulge me, eh? Sometimes I like to think I'm some kind of wise old man. I could do voiceovers like Morgan Freeman, don'tcha reckon?"

Penny and Izzy smiled politely.

He sighed. "Nobody would be happier than me to find the golden bell, but I've seen what it's done to some folks. Are obsessions ever really heathy?" He gazed into the middle distance for a long moment, then seemed to pull himself back to the present. "Tell you what though, how would you like to explore a theory?"

"A theory? Related to the golden bell? Yes please." Penny smiled.

"Well, this theory is all about the bell. You know: the actual bell part of it. You'll have seen the illustrations, all nature's glory, flowers and whatnots, yeah?"

They nodded.

"Some people think the flowers are a clue, and that it's extra fiendish because flowers are seasonal. Especially the bell flowers."

"Like bluebells!" Izzy yelled. She spun round on the spot, looking for bluebells.

"Exactly," said Geoffrey. "Barry pointed that out to me. Knows his plants, that man. Now, there are plenty of literal-minded people who go mad searching everywhere that bluebells grow. Every spring, regular as clockwork."

"Imagine doing that," said Penny, even though she had been about to suggest the very same thing.

"We can be a bit smarter than that, though. Even here. In

this field, there's a place where the bluebells grow, and it's right by a tree. Certain old maps identify the tree as Goulds Oak." Geoffrey tapped the side of his nose and winked at them.

"You're thinking Gould is gold," nodded Penny. "I take it you've searched there before?"

"I have indeed, as have others. But why not try your luck? It's the big oak in the far west corner." He pointed. "Let me show you."

The three of them scanned the earth as they walked over.

"Don't forget," said Geoffrey, "gentle side to side movements with your detectors. Like you're spreading chocolate icing on a cake."

It was only a few minutes before Penny found something. "I heard a beep," said Penny. "I think it's small, based on Davey's lesson."

Geoffrey waved his own detector over the same spot. "Could be a shotty or a grot," he said.

"Grot?" said Izzy.

"A Roman coin with no markings. You'll find them all over."

He crouched down and took a large knife from his belt, a hunting knife with a moulded grip. With it, he sawed a circle out of the turf and lifted it out.

"Look through that," he said.

As Izzy pawed through the plug of earth, he waved a smaller device over it. It beeped and whistled until Izzy had a small piece of bent metal in her hand.

"Fence staple," said Geoffrey.

"A fence staple?"

"Yep."

"I feel as though I should keep it. But I also don't want to keep it because it's rubbish."

"See how you feel by the end of the day," said Geoffrey.

The end of the day brought another fence staple, what might have been the spring from a ballpoint pen, a tiny washer and a hook.

They shared their finds with the rest of the group and were permitted to take them home as they were definitely not reportable antiquities.

Izzy was thrilled with the hook. "It's like the ones you can buy now as part of a hook and eye set. I could sew it onto a garment. How brilliant would that be?"

Penny wasn't so impressed. "But why? What makes that one better than a new one? It's got rust on it, for one thing."

"I'll soon get rid of that. Because it's got some history, it's connected to the person who wore it and lost it in that field. It's thrilling to imagine it's been waiting there in the ground and now we can use it again. How many invisible threads connect us to other people in the past like that?"

Before they were dismissed for the afternoon, Davey reminded them there was no regular meeting on Friday, it being Good Friday, but there would be another outdoor event here on Saturday. Across the way, Geoffrey gave the pair of them an encouraging look and a thumbs up.

Penny returned the thumbs up. One couldn't say no to a nice old man like that.

28

That evening, Izzy pulled up a stool to the kitchen counter so that she could watch Marcin work as he made pierogi. He had a well-practised production line so that small batches of the delicious dumplings were being constructed, boiled, then fried at the same time, moving along to make way for the next batch. Izzy tried to count how many he was making, but it wasn't easy as they were a moving target.

"Why are those ones separate?" she asked, pointing at the very first batch he'd made, set on a plate on the other side of the kitchen.

"They are vegan, so that Aubrey can try some," said Marcin. "Some of these will be snacks for tomorrow night."

"Another meeting of your secret barn club?" said Izzy. She tried to make the comment sound light-hearted, but her heart sank every time she thought about the strange chasm which had opened up between them.

"We will be finished soon enough," said Marcin.

Izzy had no idea what that meant. "Penny and I might go metal detecting again on Saturday." Changing the subject was the only sensible option if she wanted to preserve her sanity.

"Oh yes? Does it interest you?" Marcin asked, crimping dough with his hands.

Izzy pondered the question. "It's definitely an interesting pastime," she said eventually. "But I'm not all that sure if I have the right temperament to walk up and down for hours, just hoping I might find something interesting."

"Hm. That sounds like a correct assessment of the Izzy I know." Marcin smiled.

"Could you train a dog to find things?" Izzy asked.

Marcin spread his hands wide. "Many dogs are trained to find things. If they can detect the smell then they can be trained. That is why we have dogs who can sniff out drugs or explosives."

"How do they do it?" Izzy asked. "Wouldn't the dog get addicted to the drugs?"

Marcin laughed. "The dog doesn't have to consume the thing they seek. What they should be doing is performing the task their handler expects, and most of the time that means they must step back from what they have uncovered. They are rewarded with a treat when they do the job that is required of them. This reinforces the behaviour the handler wants."

"Yes, I can see that. A bomb-sniffing dog wouldn't last long if it grabbed the bomb and ran round in circles with it."

"Precisely."

Izzy's mind turned over the possibilities.

29

On Wednesday afternoon, Penny closed the shop so they could attend Sybil's funeral. As per Gwen's suggestion, they had decided to wear clothes that were colourful. Izzy wore an A-line skirt made out of purple corduroy, teamed with a green peasant blouse. Penny wore a trouser suit in pale blue with a pink silk blouse.

"Do I look too much like an Easter egg?" asked Penny with a glance in the mirror.

"It's a spring-like colour combination, definitely," said Izzy. "And now I want chocolate."

Penny scowled at her.

"You look great!" said Izzy. "Only you can dress like an Easter egg and still look amazing."

There was a certain sort of funeral that seemed to be for people who were not necessarily religiously inclined, but were culturally attached to the trappings of the church. St Michael's, always welcoming, was happy to oblige. The only hymn was *All Things Bright and Beautiful*, which always reminded Penny of primary school assemblies. The reading, delivered by Horace Atkinson, was a poem by Tennyson that Penny had never heard before. The words of one verse struck her.

AH, sad and strange as in dark summer dawns
  The earliest pipe of half-awaken'd birds
  To dying ears, when unto dying eyes
  The casement slowly grows a glimmering square;
  So sad, so strange, the days that are no more.

ON A SPRING DAY, when so many mourners had come here in gay garments to celebrate a woman's life, this poem seemed downbeat and filled with regret.

Gwen, her husband, and their three teenage children were on the front row. The Atkinsons took the spaces next to them. Barry Catchpole, looking dishevelled and heartbroken, sat in the pews behind. Others were scattered throughout the available seating. Penny saw Geoffrey from the metal detecting club, and on the opposite side of the aisle, almost in a mirror position, Dougal Thumbskill from the jigsaw shop. Even further back was Timmy with Old McGillicuddy. It was the first time Penny had ever seen the man and his dog anywhere outside the market square.

Afterwards, outside in the churchyard, Penny and Izzy waiting politely for the other mourners to emerge before they could all go up to the Community Rooms for the wake. Dougal Thumbskill approached them slowly.

"Page eleven," he said.

"Pardon?" said Izzy.

He pointed past her hip to the gravestone next to her. It was weathered and marked with lichen, but still bore a clear carving of two lifelike skulls.

"The painting on page eleven," he said.

He was right. Penny realised the gravestone was indeed the subject of one of the paintings in *The Golden Bell*.

"There's a bit on that page about Spring equinox and the sundial on the church wall," said Penny.

"There is," said Dougal. "Some have conjectured that one might see where the spire's shadow falls on that day or – and I'm not saying I've spent nights up here with string and nails – perhaps what it is those skulls' eyes are looking at."

Penny turned round, trying to angle where those hollow sockets might be gazing. "You think they are looking at the treasure?"

Dougal grunted, grimly amused. "You think I might give away clues if I thought they were the right ones?"

Penny tutted. "You're not being very helpful, are you?"

He scoffed at that. "You want help then?"

"Only if you're willing to properly offer it."

"Fine," he said, haughtily. "The clues to the golden bell treasure can be found in the pictures in the book."

"Yes?"

"Count them."

"Count them?"

"The pictures. Count them." With that he began to

wander slowly down the gravel path to the road, then left towards the Community Rooms.

The funeral party were all moving towards the wake now, and Penny and Izzy joined them. In the hall where Penny had met the metal detectorists the week before, there were now tables laid out with photos and memorabilia from Sybil's life.

"Oh hey, check out the flower arrangement," said Izzy, giving Penny a nudge.

On the next table, a floral tribute had been put out for all to admire.

"It's the golden bell."

Penny could tell Izzy was deconstructing it in her mind's eye as she circled the table, looking at it from all angles.

"It's very good, isn't it?" Penny said.

A hand touched Penny's arm and Gwen was there. "It's kaftan time," she said.

"Oh, very good," said Penny.

"I don't suppose one of you would do it?"

"Do what?" said Izzy.

"Be in the photo, I mean. Barry is in no fit mood to get involved, and my other half is the shy and retiring type. Horace and Alison are up for it, but—"

"Um, well I mean..." Penny faltered.

"Yep! Bagsy the blue one!" said Izzy with a smile.

"Goodness me, Izzy!" Penny laughed.

"What? Just make sure you get some pictures. It can go in the *Frambeat Gazette* as a *then and now* feature. It will be great!"

"Make sure you get permission for that," shouted Penny as Izzy went off to get changed.

"Oh, thank you! Once more you come to my rescue." Gwen beamed. "The plan is we get changed, then go over there where we have left the corner area clear for some pictures. We even have a stuffed monkey and a toy snake for added fun. I will let Alison and Horace know."

Izzy emerged a few minutes later wearing the blue kaftan. Gwen wore the red one, Horace the orange, and Alison the purple one. Penny realised that while a huge, patterned kaftan was a very forgiving garment, it reflected the wearer's personality. Izzy strode around, sweeping the fabric around her in colourful swirls. Alison was taller, and it hung from her in an effortless way. Horace moved like a roman senator, with much more gravitas than an orange kaftan really ought to convey. Gwen was like a robin redbreast, slightly smaller, but impossible to ignore, because of her character and the brightness of her attire.

"Thank you everybody!" called Gwen to the rest of the room. "We wanted to re-create a photograph from my parents' youth. There are copies of it around the room, so do find one if you want to help us with this. We have the four of us in our kaftans, along with a few props, and we'd welcome your help in arranging us into the best approximation of what you see there."

From wall speakers, music started up full of wah-wah guitar, trippy sounds and funky drums.

"Wow, *Flying Teapot*," said Horace, grinning. "This takes me back."

Penny wasn't sure if Flying Teapot was the name of the

song or the band, but she could certainly imagine young people on the hippie trail through Morocco enjoying these psychedelic rhythms.

There was a ripple of conversation and movement as people located the copies of the photograph. The four kaftan-wearers moved to the corner of the room and Penny saw Alison had a plush monkey toy, while Horace carried a rubber snake.

Voices started to shout out from the crowd.

"Red kaftan to the left. No, the other left!"

"Blue, you need to move to the middle, and bend away from the snake slightly."

It wasn't long before they were assembled in a way that looked like a twenty-first century version of the original. Penny snapped some pictures on her phone, and gave Izzy a thumbs-up.

Lots of other people took pictures with phones, and even some cameras, making Penny wonder who turned up to a funeral with a camera, and what else they were hoping to capture.

The photos were eventually taken and the group dispersed. Izzy came over to check Penny's phone to see the picture.

"I see what you're doing, Izzy," said Penny.

"What?"

"You're hanging on to that kaftan in the hope that Gwen might not ask for it back."

"No. Nooo. Definitely not. That would make me a bad person," said Izzy, looking away. "I'll just go and get changed, shall I?"

30

A buffet was uncovered on a side table. There were flatbreads and dip, hummus and mint yoghurt. There were grilled kebabs and platters of fruit and nuts. Penny guessed the Moroccan vibe had crept into the buffet menu, but she noticed there were also sausage rolls and pork pies, and other staples of a Suffolk buffet. She filled a plate for her and Izzy to pick at.

Raised voices caught her attention. Barry was sitting across the way, next to Geoffrey. Barry half rose from his seat, his face contorted in anger, as he spoke to his sister. Penny caught the words, "—laughingstock of yourself," come out of his mouth.

"It's all just a bit of fun," Gwen said, struggling to keep her tone light and playful.

"There's nothing fun about any of this!" her brother hissed tersely.

A hand slipped in and took a chickpea ball from Penny's plate. "What's going on?" Izzy whispered, freshly returned and out of her kaftan.

"Gwen and Barry not seeing eye to eye on the funeral celebrations," Penny whispered back.

Geoffrey reached up and put a hand on Barry's arm. It seemed as if the older man's touch served as a lightning conductor and took the rage out of Barry. He sat back down and gave a small huff of derision.

"The sooner this is over with the better," said Barry, as though that was the final word on the matter.

"Geoffrey and Barry Catchpole are good friends then?" said Izzy, observing.

Penny nodded and scooped up some hummus with a triangle of bread. "Geoffrey is a golden bell enthusiast. So Dougal Thumbskill says."

"Is that so?"

"He also says Geoffrey was in prison."

"Bit of a gossip our Dougal, isn't he?"

"He's not wrong," said Horace Atkinson.

Penny gave a start and almost dropped her lunch. She'd not heard the older man coming up beside her.

"Sorry, my dear," he said. "I didn't mean to startle you, but be warned. What you were told is right. That Geoffrey Carnarvon is a wrong one. Don't be fooled by his folksy, beardy manner, girls. He was in Driffield Prison on armed robbery charges. A life sentence, bumped up to the maximum for violent behaviour inside."

"You're very well informed," said Izzy.

"The solicitor in me," Horace smiled. "I get to see all the wrong 'uns eventually. And, trust me, a leopard never changes his spots."

None of them were talking particularly loudly, but at that moment Geoffrey turned his head to look at them, as though, across the hall, he'd heard every word they'd just said.

"Stay well clear," Horace whispered and backed away to rejoin his wife on what was rapidly becoming a retro dance floor.

Geoffrey eased his bulk up from his chair and ambled over to Penny and Izzy. "Now, what's she been telling you?" he said to Izzy.

"Er, pardon?" said Izzy.

"Has Penny been selling you on the delights of metal detecting as a hobby?"

"Oh. Oh, I see. No, she hasn't."

"Ah," he said expansively, stretching as though warming up to a subject. "She should be. A chance to connect to the land, to delve into landscape and history."

"It sounds a lot of fun," Izzy agreed.

He nodded. "I hear you've played your parts in making today a special send off for Mrs Catchpole. Good on you."

"Thank you," said Penny.

He nodded towards Horace and Alison Atkinson, who were swaying together to the psychedelic music: Alison with the rubber snake draped around her shoulders like a stole.

"But now it's done," said Geoffrey darkly. "I reckon you should stay away from the likes of them."

Izzy frowned. "Who? Them?"

"Don't be fooled by their charming middle-class 'Oh we used to be hippies' manner. Huh, snakes the pair of them. Especially him."

"Not a fan of lawyers?" suggested Izzy.

Geoffrey wagged a finger at her as though she was proving his point.

"You won't hear this from them, but right up to the day Mrs Catchpole died they were making plans to sue her."

"Sue her?"

"Sue Sybil?" said Penny in disbelief. "Whatever for?"

Geoffrey chuckled. "Trees. Trees and gardens. And snakes."

Penny and Izzy frowned at one another, then Penny looked to Geoffrey.

"Did you know Sybil thought she was going to be murdered? Or knew she had been murdered?"

"What's that?" he said.

"Or we think so," said Izzy quickly. "Suspect so. It's just a theory."

"Murdered?"

"Perhaps not an appropriate topic of conversation for a funeral," said Izzy, backtracking further.

"Murder," Geoffrey repeated, faintly, as though the idea was sinking in deeper, fading as it went.

He gave a look to each of them. Penny couldn't rightly say what kind of a look it was, but it was not a happy or a kind one.

"You will have to excuse me," he said softly and walked away. Penny noted a shaking energy in his legs as he walked off, as though he was trying to contain some terrible emotion.

"Sometimes, I think we should think before we open our mouths," said Izzy.

"Quite probably true," said Penny.

31

Izzy crashed through the door of Cozy Craft, making Penny jump.

"Sorry, arms full!" she shouted. She staggered over to the counter and put down the library books she'd been carrying.

"What's this, Izzy? I thought you'd already bought a book about different ways to cook potatoes?" Penny said as she looked at the titles.

"I can't afford to miss any. I have a mission. I need to create a menu of the finest potato recipes that it's possible to have, and make Marcin pay attention to me again."

"Oh Izzy, don't you think—?"

"—Don't. I know this is not necessarily a rational thing to do, but I don't care. If you want to help me then use your computer to organise the list, will you."

Penny was taken aback. Izzy was attempting to be

organised. This was very serious. "You want a spreadsheet? I thought you had an allergy to them or something."

Izzy scowled. "Sometimes they do the job. This feels like one of those times."

Penny beamed. "Let's do it then. Shall we organise the various recipes into groups? It will help you to identify duplicates and make sure you can create a varied menu. As varied as an entirely potato-based menu can be, anyway."

"Yep. Do your spreadsheet magic." Izzy leaned back slightly as she said the words, as if spreadsheets might be contagious.

Ten minutes later Penny had designed a spreadsheet that she thought might work. "Right. We've got some metrics we can work on to help you with your menu planning. Each recipe needs to be classified as a starter, a main, a side, or a pudding, first of all."

"We have potato puddings?"

"I think I saw a potato cake recipe in one of those books, yeah," said Penny.

"That is definitely going to make the cut. What else?"

"Well, I didn't quite know how to express this, but we need to try and give each thing a percentage potato-ness rating. Lots of things will be a hundred per cent, like mashed potatoes; but there are some where it's only part potato. Like fishcakes."

"Huh, I guess that's true. My mind was mostly on pure potato dishes, but your approach will give us more balance."

"We should also include the healthiness rating from before," said Penny.

It was quiet in the shop, so with a couple of concentrated

hours' work, the recipes from all of the books were unduplicated and catalogued using Penny's scoring system.

"That was such a great piece of work," said Penny.

"It really was," said Izzy. "I can devise a menu now, and know it's backed up with science."

"What were you thinking?" asked Penny.

"Well, it seems sensible to have a starter and a pudding based on potato, then a main with three sides."

"I like your approach – divide and conquer. How many puddings did we find in the end?" Penny asked.

"There were three, but all cakes. I think I will go for chocolate potato cake. It sounds like a winner. Something like rosti or latkes for starters, I reckon."

Penny nodded; she didn't want to interrupt Izzy's mental flow.

"Then I think a classic shepherd's pie will be a great main, with boiled new potatoes, Hasselback potatoes and Duchesse potatoes to accompany it."

"Wow, I see what you're doing there, you have a great variety of textures. We should add a texture column to the spreadsheet!" Penny pounced on the keyboard, enthused by the new dimension they had exposed.

"No, I think our analysis is complete. Thank you so much for your help. It's a great plan isn't it? It can't fail to impress."

"I'm impressed just thinking about it, Izzy," said Penny honestly.

32

"What does Maundy even mean?" asked Penny as she brought mid-morning cups of tea into the shop front.

"Excuse me?" said Izzy.

"Tomorrow's Good Friday. Today's Maundy Thursday. I'm asking what Maundy is. Is it something to do with that special money the monarch gives to poor people?"

"You came and asked the right person," said Izzy, "since it's part of my 'Word Nerd' column in the *Frambeat Gazette* this week. Maundy, from the same root as mandate or mandatory. It means a command."

"I knew you'd knew." Penny tossed Monty a little crunchy dog biscuit and sipped her tea. "Words will get us into trouble one day."

"You mean *cross words*," said Izzy, pointedly.

Penny decided her tea was too hot and put it down for a minute. "We need to make a decision."

"Whether to go to the police or not?"

"Whether to continue with the notion there was something weird about Sybil Catchpole's death. In everyone's mind it seems done and dusted. Literally. The woman has been cremated now. Her children have moved on. No one is clamouring for justice or anything."

Izzy seemed less certain. "Either the words in that crossword, her final crossword, are just part of an absolutely massive coincidence, or there was something mighty suspicious about her death."

"True. *Homicide Sybil Poison Foxglove*. So we take it that she knew she had been murdered with foxglove seeds."

"Or *Sybil Accident Poison Foxglove*. She realised she had accidentally poisoned herself."

"Either way, Dr Denise was very clear that if she'd ingested that poison she'd not have time to compose a crossword – let alone post it to the *Frambeat Gazette*."

"By the way, I'm impressed how well you get on with Denise, considering she swiped Aubrey from under your nose."

Penny scowled. "Swiped nothing. Denise and I are both adults and there plenty more fish in the sea."

"I don't see you going out with your fishing net."

"Stop changing the subject. So, Sybil couldn't have known she'd either been murdered or accidentally poisoned. Besides, the obvious thing to do would be to actually phone for help, or go to the Atkinsons next door."

"Who were suing her, according to Geoffrey Carnarvon."

"Hmmm. Then it's suicide," said Penny. "She wrote the crossword as a suicide note."

"There is a nice symmetry there," admitted Izzy.

"How so?"

"Her pen name as a crossword compiler was Socrates. The original Socrates – you know, Ancient Greece – he killed himself by drinking poison."

"Foxglove?"

"Hemlock. He'd been convicted of the crime of 'corrupting the young' of Athens."

Penny gave this some thought. "Punishing herself for her crimes?"

"But suicide doesn't appear as a word in the crossword, while homicide very clearly does. Also, it's like Alison Atkinson said: the poison was mixed into the jar of herbal tea. Leaving it there for others to potentially harm themselves? Not knowing if she was giving herself a full dose?"

"Maybe she hoped to harm others too," Penny suggested.

"That's random and cruel."

"We never really knew the woman, did we? I don't think Barry particularly liked her. The Atkinsons evidently had problems with her."

"No. It still doesn't make sense. No version of her death makes sense." Izzy took a long drink of tea. "Two words which maybe do belong together in the crossword are *accident* and *Ivor*."

"The drink-driving incident back in the eighties. That man, er, Bickerstaff?"

"Bickerthwaite. Ken Bickerthwaite," said Izzy. "I've been doing some research. And when I say 'research', I do just mean Googling things on the internet."

"Of course."

"So, Bickerthwaite was in the area looking for the golden bell. Interesting how he was on the very track leading to the Catchpole's cottage when the car hit him. I don't know if he knew she lived there."

Penny had *The Golden Bell* book on the counter and she placed her hand on it. "At least half the pictures in here are of places or geographical features in the local area. Dougal Thumbskill is a Suffolkist."

"A what?"

"That's what they call themselves, the treasure hunters who think the bell is buried in this county. Geoffrey is one too."

"Here's one thing I found out, though," said Izzy. "When he was convicted of death by dangerous driving, Ivor spent the majority of his sentence in Driffield Prison."

Penny frowned for a moment and then understood. "The same prison as Geoffrey? And—" she quickly did the mental maths "—they were there at the same time."

"Yet another coincidence?"

Penny struggled to wrap her head around it. "So – hang on. The husband of the woman who buried the golden bell – a man who possibly knew its location when she buried it – spent time in prison with a man who has now devoted the last few years of his life to finding it."

"And who is quite clearly chummy with the woman's son."

Penny puffed her cheeks out at the significance of this. "Our friend Geoffrey is very much at the heart of this thing, isn't he?"

"A man with a violent past."

"So Horace Atkinson says."

"A robber."

"A thief."

"With a lust for gold, perhaps."

They looked at one another.

"You know how some people are terrible gossips," said Izzy. "Latching onto the flimsiest titbits and spreading malicious stories about folks…"

"You think we might turn into those kinds of women?" said Penny.

"We'd best double check that we haven't already become them."

It was a sobering thought. They drank their tea silently for a time.

"Here's a thing," said Penny, pulling *The Golden Bell* book across the counter and opening it to the foreword. "Here. *This book contains sixteen pictures which tell the story of brave Sir Percival and his search for the golden bell.* Dougal Thumbskill told me to count the pictures in the book. There's fifteen."

Izzy gave her a quizzical look.

"I can count," said Penny. There are fifteen pictures. Some on a single page, some on a two-page spread. But there's definitely fifteen."

"So where's the sixteenth? Is it hidden somehow?"

"Right. A hidden picture." She opened the book wide so she could hold the mostly blank first page up to the light at the window. "I looked for a watermark."

"Have you tried that thing with lemon juice and a lit match?"

"I don't think they'd have put a lemon juice invisible ink picture in every copy of the book."

"But have you looked?"

"Do you think Annalise will fine me if I take back a library book with scorch marks on it."

"But there's a sixteenth picture somewhere!"

Penny took a deep breath and shrugged. "It's no wonder this treasure has yet to be found."

33

Izzy presented the images of the funeral kaftan fun to the *Frambeat* editorial team that evening. Glenmore sat back in his comfy chair and mushed his lips thoughtfully.

"Are such levels of fun distasteful at a funeral?" Izzy asked cautiously.

"No, no," he said softly. "I like a lively funeral. At my Aunt Abigay's funeral – Nine Night they call it back home – I drank so much white rum and danced so hard that the children found me on the beach the next day and thought I had died. My sister had to drive me, hungover and penitent, to my hotel on the other side of the island."

"Jamaica, right?" said Tariq.

"She did it out the kindness of her own heart," said Glenmore. "Yes, these are good."

"So, that's most of the pages filled," said Annalise. "Are we going to have a wordsearch again on the puzzle page? No one's complained, but it's hardly up to the level of Socrates' crosswords."

"You could have a go at writing one yourself," Tariq suggested, not for the first time.

Annalise shook her head and tutted. "There's a knack to it; a skill. I'm good at solving them, not making them. Oh, speaking of solving puzzles, I had a look at that codebreaker you sent me, Izzy." She dipped into her bag and pulled out several sheets of folded paper.

Izzy saw they were printed versions of the photos she'd taken of Sybil's coded journal and the code key at the front of the book.

"Ah, I had a go too," said Tariq. "I couldn't get anywhere with it."

"No, me neither," said Annalise. "It looks like a simple cipher: the letters of the alphabet, first in order and then jumbled. But when you apply it to the text you get more nonsense. Same if you apply it in reverse. Or apply it twice."

"So it's a tricky code?" said Izzy.

"No, I think it's nonsense," said Annalise. "Look. In the text there are several one letter words. That's basically going to be 'I' or 'A' unless there's an initial. But several different code letters are used. I even looked at the two letter words. The combinations simply can't equate to a static cipher. Either the code changes as you go through the book, which is some next-level enigma cryptography, or it's all gibberish."

Izzy wasn't particularly happy with this answer. "But it clearly says you can read the journal using that key."

Annalise shrugged. "An old woman's final joke? A puzzle that can't be solved?"

34

On Good Friday morning, Penny found a card had been shoved through the shop letterbox. An Easter card. It had a floral pattern on the front and a message inside, written in the kind of flowing script one rarely saw these days, offering thanks from Alison and Horace Atkinson for the tie-dyed kaftans and inviting Penny and Izzy to come over for tea if they wished.

Good Friday was a religious bank holiday and Izzy took such things seriously. They had no intention of opening the shop. However, a phone call confirmed that Izzy felt there was no problem with utilising the day in paying a visit to a pair of elderly town residents.

"But we have to do some training with Monty first," Izzy had said.

"What kind of training?"

"I'll explain when I come over," said Izzy and did exactly that.

Thirty minutes later, Izzy had explained her intention to give Monty a crash course in treasure finding.

"Why ... why would we do that?"

"Easter eggs, golden bells, lost car keys. How cool would it be if we had a dog that could find buried things, huh?"

Penny was sceptical. "You're sure Marcin said this would work?"

"Pretty much," said Izzy.

"Pretty much, she says."

"Sceptic."

"Hmmm. I'm wondering if this counts as a new crazy project. Lent still has two more days."

"This is not a project. It's a plan. And anyway, since someone stole those fleeces from under my nose, my crazy project mojo has taken a bit of a hit."

"Says the woman who is planning a crazy potato banquet for her boyfriend."

"That's cooking. That's different."

"Really?"

"Really."

"Fine," said Penny. "We can spend a little while training Monty, then we're off for tea with the Atkinsons."

"Monty and I won't be long."

"Oh, I think I might come with you. I need to see this in action," said Penny. "So you're saying you hide the treats in the ground and Monty is therefore motivated to dig for treasure?"

"Yes, that! Exactly that."

"Surely he will just be motivated to dig holes?" Penny

said as they left the shop. "I can't quite see how he will make the leap to finding treasure or Easter eggs."

"Because he is very clever," said Izzy. "You know how he listens to our conversations and seems to understand loads more than he ought to? I reckon he will put it all together like the Wonder Dog he really is."

They walked up Church Street with Monty sniffing everything as he always did. Izzy had been around earlier and hidden some treats. They were coming up to the first one, which was in the corner of a flower bed. A few yards ahead of them, a handsome spaniel sniffed at the edge of the bed.

"No!" Izzy hissed under her breath. She hadn't considered the possibility of other dogs detecting the hidden treats. The spaniel walked on without investigating further and Izzy relaxed.

"Oh hey, Monty, what's here?" she said in an exaggerated voice when they got to the flower bed. "Could there be some buried treasure?" She danced ahead of him, directing his nose to the right spot.

Monty paused for a moment, slightly confused, then he raised his nose and sniffed the air. He tugged to the side and put his nose to the soil in the flower bed.

"Good boy, Monty. He has the scent!" Izzy crowed. "Go on boy, dig it up!"

Monty didn't need to be asked twice. He scrabbled wildly at the edge of the flower bed, sending soil across the pavement. He soon had a hole that was twice as deep as the treat had been buried, and he seemed to realise his mistake as he lost the scent for a moment. He raised his head before homing in on the treat, which he'd flung across the pavement. He gobbled it up, victorious.

"Success!" Izzy yelled.

"I'm not sure I would call it that," said Penny. "There is soil everywhere! If Stuart Dinktrout saw us doing this he would have a thousand fits."

Izzy used the side of her foot to shovel the soil roughly back into place, though almost certainly not to the satisfaction of Stuart Dinktrout, chair of the local chamber of commerce. "There, it's not too bad. Come on, let's find more treasure, Monty. You're a very clever boy, aren't you?"

Izzy gave Monty lots of fuss, making sure to reinforce the good behaviour.

They continued on their way, excavating dog treats from flower beds, then from beneath the turf near to the castle.

"He can't dig here!" Penny said, horrified.

"It's already loose from where I buried the treat," said Izzy. "We can stomp it back into place when we're done. It's good practice for him surely? Treasure won't always be conveniently buried in loose soil."

Penny hovered anxiously while Monty made a jagged scar in the neat green grass. He recovered the treat and Izzy repaired the hole using her feet, then her hands, in an attempt to get all of the soil back under the turf.

"This walk is making me a nervous wreck. How many more treats are buried?" asked Penny.

"Only another six," said Izzy. "Monty should definitely know what he's doing by then."

In the early afternoon, with the sun high in the sky and

providing almost summer-like warmth, they walked together to the Atkinson's house.

This was the first time either of them had seen the property up close from the front, rather than from Sybil's garden to the rear, and it was a significantly larger property than Avalon Cottage.

"Clearly soliciting pays well," said Izzy and pressed the old-style brass doorbell.

"Do not be deceived," said Horace Atkinson popping round from a bush to the side of the house. "The whole place is falling down, I can assure you."

"I'm sorry. Didn't see you there," said Izzy, her cheeks flushing pink.

"Oh, I love overhearing an unguarded conversation," Horace grinned. "Come through, come through." He was wearing a wide-brimmed straw hat and pale loose cotton clothes, as though dressed for farmwork in some sweltering equatorial country, rather than pottering around an English garden.

Round the back of the house a table had already been set out for tea on the lawn.

"Expecting us then?" said Penny.

"Oh, we find it's always easier to expect guests all the time," said Alison, emerging from the house with a tea tray laden with toasted and buttered hot cross buns. "That way we're always prepared."

"And if no one appears then it's double the cake for me!" said Horace with a roguish glint in his eye.

35

Alison insisted on pouring, even though the pot was heavy and her hands shook. The hot cross buns were perfectly toasted, and the melted butter glistened on their crisped surface.

"There's only one thing I don't like about hot cross buns," said Alison.

"Do the currants get stuck between your teeth?" said Izzy, wiggling a tongue behind her lip.

Alison laughed, polite rather than amused. "What I find infuriating is that the moment Christmas is over, they start stocking them in the supermarkets. Christmas done? Boom! Hot cross buns!"

"Easter eggs too," said Horace. "Who needs to buy an Easter egg in February?"

"There's only one day to eat hot cross buns," said Alison, "and that day is today."

"And the weird new flavours," said Horace in his best appalled voice. "Salted caramel hot cross buns? Chocolate and lime hot cross buns? It's consumer choice gone mad."

Penny smiled. She couldn't help but agree the supermarkets seemed to lurch from one season to the next. From Christmas to Easter, to summer holidays and barbecues, to Halloween, and back to Christmas. However, she'd tried a salted caramel hot cross bun only the other week and thought it delicious. "Well, these are very nice," she said.

Over their second cup, Alison said, "You've both been very helpful to Gwen of late." There was something about the way the older woman dropped it in the conversation that made Penny think this was the very purpose of the Atkinsons' inviting them over.

"We just like making things," said Izzy.

"And charging for our services," Penny added.

"The bears, the kaftans. It's meant a lot to her," said Alison.

"Glad to help."

"And I wonder if you could have a word with her on our behalf."

Izzy frowned. "You're good friends with her, aren't you?"

"Things have become a little strained of late," said Horace, reaching for the bowl of sugar cubes.

"You seemed to get on famously at the funeral though."

"The very British skill of maintaining a polite and diplomatic front. We love Gwen dearly. She's like the daughter we never had. Her children, like grandchildren to us."

"But there is a small and on-going bone of contention," said Alison. "Or tree."

Penny immediately looked to her left and the ash tree which stood in the corner of Sybil's old garden, looming over the Atkinsons' lawn.

"I do not know what Gwen and Barry wish to do with the house, but with Sybil, um, laid to rest, I feel it's time to address these problems. The roots have damaged our house. Are *still* damaging our house."

"I could simply pop round with a chainsaw in the middle of the night—" said Horace.

"You'll do no such thing," Alison interrupted him.

"—But we want to resolve this amicably."

"Very understandable."

"Aren't Ivor's mum's ashes buried there?" said Izzy.

"Susan? No. Ashes scattered at Dunwich beach I seem to recall. The plaque is just a plaque: a memorial to a grandmother Gwen and Barry never even remembered. Her death hit Ivor very hard, a big contributor to his alcoholism."

"The plaque is a memorial. Such things can mean a lot to people."

"Meaning be damned," said Horace. "We want our house protected from that tree. Repaired even. *Restitutio in integrum.*"

"A little bird told me you were contemplating challenging Sybil legally over that tree," said Izzy.

Horace laughed but there was a bitterness in him now. "Was that a little jailbird by any chance?"

"I'm sorry," said Izzy. "I didn't mean to offend."

"Especially while we're eating your delicious hot cross buns," said Penny.

Horace smiled at this. "Never get old, Penny. Never retire. You end up with too much time on your hands to dwell on things. The molehills of the mind become mountains. That tree is just a tree; but it is affecting our happiness."

"I don't know why Gwen is so resistant to us taking it down," said Alison.

"But my warnings about Geoffrey Carnarvon remain true," said Horace. "Did you know he went to prison with our friend, Ivor?"

"We kind of figured it out," said Izzy.

"In fact, he was Ivor's cellmate at the end. When he killed himself."

"An accident surely," said Penny.

"Don't be so certain. Ivor was a gentle loving soul. Flawed like the rest of us, for sure, but he was not a criminal, and he was not cut out for prison life."

"You think it was suicide then?"

"Perhaps," said Horace. "Did you know that very shortly after his release, Geoffrey came here, to this house?"

"He did," said Alison. "This was maybe twenty years ago. We didn't know who he was at the time, but when he told us it chilled us to the bone. That's twice I've said bones now. Must have bones on the brain."

"And indeed, Geoffrey made no bones about the reason for his visit," said Horace. "He was interested in the treasure. Said he had known Ivor in prison and had decided to come visit the area where Geoffrey had lived, and where the fabulous treasure was buried. He had a copy of the book right there in his hand."

"Ivor would have known where the golden bell was buried, right?" said Penny.

"If he did, that was something he and Sybil kept between themselves. But then Geoffrey's questioning took a sinister turn. Do you remember, dear?"

"Oh, yes," said Alison. "He started asking about the letters."

"What letters?" said Penny, her mind turning to the jumbled-up letters of the encoded journal.

"Exactly," said Alison. "He wanted to know about the 'letters' Ivor had sent from prison. We knew nothing about any such things. And then he said something odd. He wanted to know why Ivor hadn't been released."

"He was only partway through his sentence," said Horace, "but he was adamant—"

"Angry too."

"—Angry and adamant that the letters would have secured Ivor's release."

"He's a big and intimidating man is Geoffrey," said Alison.

"I wasn't personally afraid," Horace put in.

"But he was bigger and younger and more intimidating twenty years ago, and we did not care for his tone at all. We told him to clear off and never come bothering us again."

"I called the police. Sergeant Gascoigne it was back then," said Horace. "You can never get hold of an actual policeman these days, but back then you knew the bobbies in the town by name. I made sure the coppers put a flea in his ear, but clearly they didn't give him a stern enough warning..." Horace sighed. "The absolute villain has hung around Fram ever since."

"Such things are sent to try us," said Alison and then put on a smile. "Now, who's for more tea?"

36

It was a slow and thoughtful walk back from the Atkinson's house to the little shop in Framlingham.

"You know what I think?" said Penny eventually.

"What?" said Izzy.

"If we're looking for an explanation of how Sybil died, then Geoffrey Carnarvon very much fits the bill."

"How so?"

"What is it that the police say? Means, motive and opportunity. He clearly has a motive: he wants to get hold of the golden bell."

"We know that, do we?"

"He has a copy of the book. He moved to the area quite deliberately twenty years ago. He is a metal detectorist."

"So, he has an interest in all things buried then."

"He's a convicted armed robber."

Izzy grunted.

"What?" said Penny. "The man literally went to prison for seeking wealth and resorting to violence and threats to do so. That is precisely what armed robbery is."

"You've met him," said Izzy. "He's a big, chubby, white-bearded old gentleman."

"You think that because he looks like Father Christmas, he can't be a bad person?"

"Your theory that he did it is based upon his past."

"And ... how's this for a scenario? What if, last year, Geoffrey went to Sybil's house because he wanted the golden bell."

"Okay..."

"He goes in, breaks in even, and threats Sybil. A defenceless, ill, older woman would be frightened of this man. And ... he threatens her. He puts the foxglove seeds in her jar of dried tea and mixes it up and tells her he's going to poison her if she doesn't tell him where the golden bell can be found."

"So, she's being threatened with poisoned tea?"

"Right! So that means that while he's there, she's still sort of got time to write a crossword."

Izzy frowned. "So, it's sort of 'Excuse me, Mr Burglar-Man, could I just make some notes and write out a crossword while you stand there?'"

"Okay. Okay. So, he comes in, mixes the threatening tea and says, 'Right, darlin', you'd better be ready to talk when I come back or it's the deadly tea for you, me dear.'"

"Is that your Geoffrey impression?"

"It's my sort of generic bloke impression. So he leaves her. For a day or a week. And she's worried, but she wants to get word out. So she writes the crossword and posts it, and when he comes back several days later, she still refuses to tell him, so he makes up that fatal brew and forces her to drink it."

Izzy politely gave it some thought. Up in the trees along the lane, a chiffchaff was heartily singing its two-tone song.

"Geoffrey was convicted of armed robbery," she said.

"Exactly," said Penny.

"And he went to prison."

"Where he met Ivor."

"Prison was his punishment for the crimes he must have committed more than half a lifetime ago."

"But do people ever really change?" said Penny.

Izzy looked sideways at her cousin. "It's Good Friday, you know."

"Um, I know."

"And some people would say that two thousand years ago, a certain Palestinian carpenter died on Good Friday so that people who had done wrong could ask for forgiveness for their crimes and find salvation."

Penny sighed. "Yes, but..."

"But?" said Izzy, quick and hard. "But what? Are you saying people can never escape their pasts?"

Penny didn't argue, but simply said, "I think people struggle to shrug off past sins. What's done is done."

Izzy didn't pursue it any further and they walked in cool but companionable silence for several minutes until they reached the pavement nearer the town centre.

"I have an alternative theory I think we should return to," said Izzy.

"Oh?" said Penny.

"The clues in the crossword. *Botanical, garden, homicide.*"

"The Atkinsons and the argument over the tree?"

Izzy tilted her head meaningfully and added nothing more.

37

Penny and Izzy walked to Aldham Farm at Saturday lunchtime. Monty was on high alert as they were taking an unusual route, and the early spring had brought blackbirds out to defend their territory every few yards. Penny was always impressed with the boldness of some birds in facing down a dog.

Davey was once again manning the sign-in table.

"You'll have to buy yourself your own metal detector soon," he said as he passed one over.

"Can we not keep borrowing one?" said Izzy.

He gave her a strange smile. "You don't properly connect to the earth unless it's your own detector. You don't want to go around feeling things with other people's hands."

"Are you saying a metal detector becomes an extension of your body?"

"Very much so," he said emphatically, as though such a thing was obvious.

They stepped out into the field together as one.

"This is nice, isn't it?" said Penny. The grassy field stretched ahead, with huge amounts of space for them to explore among the detectorists already there. "Keep an eye out for Geoffrey."

"So you can accuse him of murdering Sybil Catchpole?"

Penny tutted. "So we can talk to him. Generally."

Izzy made a doubtful noise and moved on.

"You know, these are not as heavy as I thought they would be," said Izzy, waving the detector. "I thought maybe you needed a harness to take the weight, but they are really quite light."

A few minutes later, Izzy paused when her detector made a sound. "Ooh, exciting! I found something." She knelt down to the ground.

Monty came running over and started to dig. He tore through the turf in a moment and then his paws were a blur as he showered Penny and Izzy with soil.

"Monty, stop!" Penny said, but it was too late. Monty had created a hole as big as himself. He sat in it, tongue lolling to the side as he gazed up at Izzy.

"What on has gone on here?" The tweed-wearing Leslie came over, pointing at the ground. "We're digging for artefacts, not tunnelling to Australia."

"Monty got a bit over-enthusiastic," said Penny.

"I've been training him," said Izzy.

"To help in metal detecting?"

"To find Easter eggs."

"Well then you shouldn't have brought him. We can't

have this kind of mess. As I always say, we are detectorists, but we like to make our presence here—"

"—Undetectable," chorused Penny and Izzy.

"Yes. Undetectable to the landowner." The woman looked deflated that she'd been robbed of her weak joke.

"But look, he found this!" Izzy picked something out of the scattered soil and held it up. It was a shiny D-shaped ring. "Look, it's a part of a dog collar. No wonder he got distressed – he was probably thinking a dog got hurt. He's very sensitive to the pain of others."

Leslie made a distrustful face but then relented. "Tidy up this hole and make sure it doesn't happen again."

They did their best to make the hole invisible.

Penny raised an eyebrow at Izzy. "Let me look at that fragment of dog collar again."

"Why?"

"It's really shiny for something that just came out of the ground. It's a lot like the one that came off Monty's old collar last week. *Very* shiny."

Izzy nodded. "It is, isn't it?"

Penny knew Izzy had performed some sleight of hand to get Monty off the hook, but before she could comment she saw Barry Catchpole nearby bent to the earth to investigate a find. Unfortunately, Monty spotted the action at the same time and with a joyous yipping sound he ran, full pelt, to assist with the excavation of the treasure.

"Monty!" Penny yelled.

She and Izzy ran over, but they were not fast enough to stop Monty digging a sizeable hole at Barry's feet, much to his annoyance.

"Sorry! So very sorry!" Penny hurried over and clipped Monty to the lead. She tugged him out of the way so that he couldn't do any more digging.

"Your dog is a menace," Barry said.

"Sorry. If we'd known he was going to be such a metal detecting fanatic we'd have left him at home."

Barry knelt and brought out a smaller wand detector from his belt to scan the spoil heap of his hole.

"Cute enough dog, I suppose," he grunted begrudgingly.

"Monty has his moments," said Penny.

"What's Monty short for?" he said.

"Cos he's got little legs," said Izzy, who couldn't resist such silliness.

"Nothing. He's just Monty," said Penny. "Not Montgomery or anything."

Barry nodded and brushed soil away from a clod of earth in his hand. "Barry's not my real name, you know. Made the decision to shorten it."

"Barrington?" suggested Penny.

He laughed. "As if. Ambrosius."

"I beg your pardon," said Izzy.

"Ambrosius. Guinevere and Ambrosius our parents christened us. Well, not christened. Named in a woodland naming ritual."

"Hippies?" said Penny.

"At least five years too late to be proper hippies. But yeah. Still, I suppose if you're parents give you a name, give you anything, you should treasure it."

The earth had been cleaned away. In his hand he held a muddy key, a simple slender yale key.

"Ooh, a find," said Izzy.

He grunted again and from his satchel took a big ring on which dozens of similar keys were threaded. He looped this new one onto the ring.

"Just think of all those doors lacking keys," said Izzy. "Do you try them out on doors you go by?"

"What?" he said.

"Your keys. If I had a big bunch of keys like that I think I would try them out on strange doors."

"Hoping to open a doorway to a magical world?" Penny suggested.

"A quick route to getting arrested more like," said Barry. "I don't have any compulsion to reunite these with their owners. Keys are just keys, nothing more, nothing less. Having hippies for parents has taught me that the world is often far less magical than you'd believe."

Mention of parents prompted Penny to think of Sybil and Ivor Catchpole, and by extension, Geoffrey. She looked round.

"I've not seen Geoffrey here today," she said.

"Don't think he's here," said Barry.

Monty sniffed around Barry's feet as he carefully pushed the soil back into the hole he'd dug.

"I wonder if you could help us with something," said Izzy. "Yes?"

"Geoffrey asked Horace Atkinson about some letters."

"Pardon?"

"Geoffrey was in prison with your dad, all those years ago. You knew that, didn't you?"

He straightened up and looked at her. "I don't— I don't

like talking about my dad, miss. Not with strangers. But, yes, I found out only recently. They were in prison together."

"And Geoffrey asked Horace about some letters that should have secured your dad's release. That struck us as odd. I couldn't imagine what it meant."

Penny could see Barry was finding the conversation distasteful, unpleasant even. "You would have to ask Geoffrey about that. I—" He turned as though about to storm off, but stopped himself and turned back to face them.

A peculiar change came over his face: a forced switch from a scowl to something softer. Penny judged it wasn't because he was trying to deceive them, but because he wanted to recognise the turmoil within himself and address it.

"I think you need to understand something about my dad," he said. "Regular kids have regular dads. I barely remember mine. Whereas most people have memories and images of their dads, I have something very different. An account of a man, an alcoholic, who was selfish and thoughtless enough to drunkenly drive into another man and kill him. I have this idea, this concept of a man who went to prison, never wrote to us, never wanted us as visitors. I have the knowledge that my dad drank himself to death, and a funeral we didn't attend."

He tapped his own chest, then pointed to Izzy and Penny.

"When you think of your own dads, you're probably thinking of a man who loved you, who always wanted you, who would have done anything to protect your mums and you. Yes?"

"Yes," said Penny, softly, guiltily.

"I should have had that. All my life, I should have had that. I didn't. In that same place, in my heart, I had something hollow and nasty. So you'll forgive me if I don't seem interested in letters, or what happened in the past."

He swallowed hard and there was a terrible dark grief in his eyes that Penny couldn't help feeling herself.

"It's like those – those damned memory bears you made for Gwen's children." He laughed. "Oh, the craftsmanship is lovely. You did a good job. But each of them is only made of fragments: pieces that are twisted to a new purpose. That's all we're left with. Twisted fragments. And maybe Gwen is happy with that. She's just the kind who can take the fragments she likes and twist them into something she can hold and love. Not me."

He lifted his detector up. "Now, if you'll forgive me, I'm going to go over there, far away, and do a bit of detecting by myself. I don't think I will bump into you again, will I?"

38

Izzy and Penny stayed silent as he walked away.

"Are we bad people?" said Izzy.

"We're bad people," said Penny and would have said more, but Monty abruptly yanked on his lead. Before she could recover he had dragged her a dozen paces downhill and plunged into the delicate hole a man was uncovering. Paws that were usually no faster than a leisurely stroll were a blur in the rich loamy soil, throwing up a spray of mud and turning the fist-sized hole into a something considerably larger.

The disturbed detectorist recoiled with a gasp of alarm.

"Monty! Monty!" Penny pulled him back. Monty, generally the most placid of dogs, struggled as she pulled. His little face was one of happy eagerness: to dig deeper and uncover goodies.

The detectorist was waving his detector over the hole and

shaking his head. "Could have been gold!" he hissed to himself.

Penny could see tweedy Leslie and organiser Davey coming at them from different angles.

"Really sorry!" Penny called out to them. "I had him on the lead."

"Could have been Saxon gold!" the detectorist was muttering.

"This is not acceptable behaviour!" said Leslie.

"I think we need to draw a line under this..." said Davey.

"I was dirt fishing for Saxon gold," said the detectorist.

"First up, it's not Saxon gold, Colin," said Davey. "Secondly, we're not dirt fishers, please. Thirdly—"

"You and your dog need to go," said Leslie firmly.

Davey looked like he was going to disagree, then tilted his head.

"Four-legged friends are a hindrance not a help in the field of detecting. Your friend can stay, but you need to go."

Penny nodded and looked at Izzy.

Izzy shook her head. "We were doing it together."

"Well, the dog needs to go," said Davey. Leslie did a sort of Miss Piggy harrumph in agreement, as though those were the very words she had wanted to say.

"I trained him to do this," said Izzy. "I'll go."

"He's my dog," said Penny.

"Our dog, surely. He lives in our shop."

"Where I live," said Penny.

The two of them looked at each other, then at the put-out detectorists.

"We'll both go," said Izzy.

"We're really sorry," said Penny.

"Hope you find your Saxon gold," Izzy added to Colin.

Together, chastised, they walked up to the field entrance and the table where they could return their detector.

Penny and Izzy ambled slowly back towards the town. They walked in silence for much of the way, for there was little to say that wouldn't remind them of how selfish their words and actions had been. They let the walk and the cool afternoon breeze wash the guilt from them.

It felt as though there was something in the air – and not just the thought of tomorrow being Easter, with the added promise of chocolate eggs, and the end to Lent vows. Below the earth and in the air, spring was definitely springing; indeed had quite possibly already sprung. The hedgerows were crowded with green and the almost entirely invisible movement of new life. Monty, whose nose and curiosity seemed indefatigable, sniffed in every hole and at every potential nesting spot.

"Odd that Geoffrey was not there today," said Penny.

"He could just have had a cold, or simply didn't feel like it," said Izzy, then gave Penny a knowing look. "Or do you think he feared Detective Penny Slipper was onto him?"

Penny raised her chin as though placing herself above cheap shots at her pet theory.

"Shall I tell you why Geoffrey Carnarvon didn't murder Sybil Catchpole?" said Izzy.

"If you wish."

"It doesn't even need refuting—"

"Good word."

"—Thank you – because it doesn't even make sense. If he

was threatening to poison Sybil, then he would appear in the crossword. He doesn't. And again – and this is the big stumbling block with any theory – if Sybil had time to write a warning note in a crossword, then she had time to make a phone call. As much as I love puzzles, a crossword is a terrible way to send a message to people."

Penny sighed, not in disagreement, but because it was true. "And yet his link to both Ivor and the treasure ... it feels so pertinent."

"Good word."

"Thank you." Penny looked at the rosy evening sky, perhaps for inspiration. "What was that business about the letters?"

"Letters?"

"Mmm. You remember what Horace and Alison were saying. Geoffrey, after coming out of prison, had visited them and demanded to know why Ivor hadn't been released."

"Right," said Izzy. "Some letters that should have guaranteed it."

Penny frowned. "What kinds of letters could possibly free a man from prison? And why would Ivor's old neighbour be the one to know about it?"

"Horace was the family solicitor. New evidence?"

"It's a drink driving case. He was drunk. He hit a man. There's not much evidence required."

"Or some legal loophole."

"But then Horace hadn't received any letters. Or, if he had, lied to Geoffrey and now to us about them."

There were no answers to be gained from speculating and questioning the evening sky. They came to the fork in the road where they would go their separate ways: Izzy to her new home with Marcin, Penny to her flat above the Cozy Craft shop.

"There is one explanation as to why Sybil appeared to be murdered, but was able to make her final accusations in a crossword," said Penny.

"Oh?"

"It was suicide, but she wanted it to look like murder."

"Huh?"

"She killed herself. She knew how she was going to die because she arranged it."

"We've discussed suicide before."

"Her motive for suicide was her debilitating and worsening illness; but maybe she had scores to settle. The fatal tea left in the jar, and the crossword, are clues to a murderer who doesn't actually exist."

Izzy thought on it. "It's interesting. Are you suggesting Sybil wanted to frame someone for her death?"

"Perhaps."

"That is a cold and callous motivation."

"You and I never really knew Sybil Catchpole – but what *do* we know? She was an ambitious and independent woman in her youth. Then how did Alison describe her...? Self-centred and increasingly bitter. She was clearly estranged from her son, Barry. Poor man. And she'd fallen out big time with the neighbours and closest friends."

"Scores to settle."

Penny made a long contemplative hum. "So, perhaps we need to ask ourselves: who did Sybil Catchpole hate? Who did she hate so much she would pin a murder on them?"

A momentary chill wind blew past, a reminder that if spring was here, there were still a few pockets of winter still around.

"I will see you tomorrow," said Izzy.

"And we'll see how many eggs our highly trained egg-snuffler will find," said Penny.

Monty looked up, sensing he was being talked about, and licked his own muddy nose. Penny turned towards town and Izzy towards her home.

39

Crazy project or not, Izzy was looking forward to cooking her potato extravaganza.

She found she was very grateful for Penny's help with spreadsheets and planning documents, as she peeled all of the potatoes in one go, rather than having to consult six recipes and peel them at different times. It meant she could double up on some other tasks as well. She soon had the kitchen filled with bowls and saucepans containing potato dishes.

The cake went into the oven first, so that it could cool for later, and the smell kept her company as she powered through the recipes.

Marcin appeared as the shepherd's pie went into the oven. She gave him a huge grin as he looked around at what probably appeared to be a huge mess.

"I am preparing us a very special meal for this evening,"

said Izzy. "It might look like a disaster zone at the moment, but we're in the eye of the storm. It will get better."

Marcin gave her a hug. "I look forward to it, tell me if I can help."

Izzy finished off the cooking and set the table.

Penny had also made menu cards, insisting it would underline the fun of the evening, so Izzy put them on the table.

She called Marcin and made a small *ta-da!* motion. "Welcome to tonight's special meal of potatoes in six ways!"

Marcin read the menu card and then laughed loudly. "Oh Izzy, this is quite amazing. Let's eat, I cannot wait to try this."

They tucked into the latkes, which were topped with apple sauce, then Izzy fetched the Shepherd's pie.

"Would you please fetch the potatoes, Marcin?" she asked. "They are on the side."

Izzy sat back, feeling slightly smug, as Marcin trailed back and forth bringing in potato dishes.

"I see what you are doing here Izzy," he said as he fetched the last of them. "This is a generous idea, but you are also making a point I think. If this is an attempt to make me eat so many potatoes that I will get sick of them, I warn you now it will not work."

Izzy laughed. "No, not at all. I wanted to make you sit up and take notice of me. It feels as though you have been a bit absent in recent weeks."

Marcin put down the dishes and reached for Izzy's hands across the table. "I am sorry if you feel neglected. It was truly not my intention."

The meal was a triumph. Izzy had been worried the potato overload would be too much, but apparently they both had an appetite for potatoes more than enough for the job.

"Potato cake is a particular triumph," said Marcin. "Today I am grateful to you for taking so much trouble over a meal, and I am also grateful to learn I can eat potatoes in a cake."

"Before you get too carried away with gratitude," said Izzy. "I should warn you about the amount of clearing up needed in the kitchen."

He started to smile, but it faded abruptly. "Izzy?"

"Yes?"

"We have been living together for two weeks."

"Yes. I suppose we have," she said.

"And you have made a lot of sacrifices – and a lot of potato dishes! – to try and make me happy."

Izzy didn't like the use of the word 'try' in that sentence.

"And I—" he continued, uncomfortably. "I have been absent and distant. And ... I have not been honest with you."

"Oh?" she said. There was a yawning pit in her stomach where there should have been nothing but potato.

"I have a confession to make. Tomorrow. I will make a confession to you and show you something."

Her mind went to the barn, and the mad, irrational, and unjustified thoughts of what kinds of secrets a man could keep locked up in such a place. "Tomorrow? Not now?"

"No," he said. "It must be tomorrow. Perhaps in the morning."

"I've got church. It's Easter Sunday."

"Of course..."

"And then I promised Penny I would go with her and Monty on the Easter egg hunt."

"Yes. Yes. After that."

"Not now though?"

"Not now," he said and took both her hands in his. "And I hope you will forgive my secrecy and my foolishness. Your hands are trembling."

"I'm sure they're just cold," she said.

40

After the Easter Sunday service at St Michael's, Izzy called in on Penny and Monty so they could all take a walk out to the Easter egg Hunt. Her mind had been unsettled since the night before. Marcin's words about confession and secrets and forgiveness had worried away at her. In church, she had sought solace in song and community. By the time she met with Penny, her mood had not necessarily lifted, but she was able to put her worst suspicions from her mind.

It was a cool and sunny afternoon, which was perfect for a walk, and as they strolled along lanes that were quieter than usual, the springtime chatter of birds in the hedgerows was a joy to hear.

"If we could understand what they were saying, do you think we'd like it as much?" asked Izzy. "The birds I mean. Aren't they all basically shouting 'Get out of my space!' and 'Check out my feathers, you'll want to mate with me!'?"

"Don't forget 'Watch out everyone, large predators coming along the path!'," said Penny. "Luckily for us, it just sounds like a delightful symphony of spring."

They arrived at Brick Lane copse, where the Easter egg Hunt was being hosted. The wooded area itself was quite small, but it backed onto a wide green space near the edge of the town. Several cars were pulled up on the roadside, and there was a gated fence where they entered the trail through woodland.

A woman who might have been one of the local primary school teachers, sold them a trail map at the entrance. It showed where the eggs might be found on a circular walk.

"We didn't bring a spade!" Izzy gasped. "How will we dig them up?"

"If it's mainly for children, I don't think it should be that challenging," said Penny. "We'll soon see. Look over there. Can I see Annalise from the library?"

Further along the trail was a small group of people, with children milling about them. Loud shrieks of delight came through the trees. Izzy thought Annalise was one of the adults, but they moved on out of sight.

"Good morning!"

An Easter bunny stepped out onto the trail. Obviously it was a person in an outfit, but it was a very good one, with a large, sculpted headpiece obscuring their face. Monty wasn't impressed. He barked at the rabbit, but only in a half-hearted way because he clearly knew he wasn't going to win in a fight.

"I love your suit," said Izzy, walking all around to check every angle.

"Thank you, Miss King," said the bunny.

The bunny clearly knew her name, but Izzy couldn't quite place the male voice.

"Now you will have seen that this is station number one on your map," he said. "Well done for getting here! I can stamp your map to say you have visited."

Penny offered the map to the rabbit, who dabbed it with a self-inking stamp.

"Now, if you would care to look behind that tree over there, you might be able to find some eggs!"

The rabbit turned to indicate a tree. When Penny and Izzy looked, they found two small chocolate eggs set on a small table.

"Thank you, rabbit!" yelled Izzy and tore open the wrapping.

"This is much more civilised than I had eggspected," said Penny.

"Is that supposed to be a yolk?" asked Izzy, chomping on her egg.

"It's organised so that everyone gets an egg. We don't need to be..." Penny made a rotating motion with her hands, indicating Izzy should provide the punchline.

Izzy rolled her eyes and continued to eat her egg.

"Come on Izzy, we don't need to be..."

"Am I supposed to say shellfish? Because that is a terrible pun," spluttered Izzy.

"Where's Monty?" Penny asked, looking all around.

"Over there." Izzy pointed. "Digging what looks like a massive hole."

They ran over to where Monty was digging. "Stop it,

Monty. We don't need to dig them up here."

Monty ignored all attempts to stop him. He had dug a hole which hid him from view by the time Penny and Izzy reached him. As Penny leaned down to clip on his lead and drag him out, Izzy held up a hand.

"Wait! He's found something." Izzy reached into the hole and grabbed something that felt like metal. She pulled and it came loose. "It's an old horseshoe! Great going, Monty!"

The rabbit had followed them over and leaned in. "A good find. We would not normally encourage digging, as it's not that kind of Easter egg Hunt, but your dog is cute."

"And we trained him to find treasure! It's really worked!" Izzy crowed.

"Has it really worked, or was that just a coincidence?" Penny asked.

They continued round the walk. The next station was supervised by someone wearing a fluffy chick outfit. As soon as they caught sight of it in the distance, Izzy started to imagine how she would make something similar.

"Oh, look at the shape of it! It's got a huge wobbly bottom half, which is what makes it look so very cute. I think it must be suspended on shoulder straps inside, with something like a hoop around the widest part so that it doesn't collapse inwards."

"Look!" whispered Penny. "The chick is peeping to see how many of us are in the group, then hiding the right number of eggs, so that it's fair for everyone."

"Spoiler alert!" said Izzy. "I thought it was all done by magic."

"Good morning!" said the chick. "Shall I stamp your map

to show that you've been here? You might find some chocolatey treats over by that bush."

As they walked away, Izzy realised something. "They stamp the map so we can't sneak round through the woods and get another set of eggs."

"Would people really do that?" Penny asked.

"I was just wondering if it might be possible," admitted Izzy.

The walk was an easy half-mile in total, and Izzy and Penny stopped for a chat with an egg person, a lamb person, and a cartoonish shepherdess at the end who turned out to be Gwen.

"Well done for finding all of the stations, and collecting a full set of stamps," said Gwen, taking their maps. "You have both earned your final prizes." She retrieved a larger egg for each of them. "Thank you so much for coming along. This woodland is very special and it needs taking care of."

Three teenagers came along the track behind them: two boys and a girl. Izzy's first thought was that the trio were a bit old for Easter egg hunts, or at least too old to enjoy as children; and perhaps too young to enjoy it as playful adults. This thought was compounded by the bored, or indeed surly expressions they wore. Izzy's second thought was that they seemed familiar in some way. She realised why when they came up to Gwen at the final table.

"Done. Eggs. Now," said the youngest.

"Please," suggested Gwen.

"We have completed your task, mother," said the tall girl in a manner that was polite, but only just.

Gwen smiled primly and passed each a larger egg.

"These are the women who made your memory bears," said Gwen, gesturing to Penny and Izzy.

"Ah," said one.

"Great," said another without enthusiasm.

"This is Mary, Joseph and little Donkey then," said Penny. "Donny – I mean Donny! Sorry."

The youngest, thunder-faced little Donny gave Penny an even darker look and the three moved off with their prizes.

"I'm so sorry," said Penny but Gwen was paying no attention. She was watching her children walking away, a soft, maternally loving look on her face.

"Children are wonderful, aren't they?" she said.

"They can be," said Izzy neutrally.

"We'd do anything for them though, wouldn't we? Either of you hoping for the pitter-patter of tiny feet soon?" asked Gwen.

"Only these ones," said Penny, jiggling Monty's lead.

Penny and Izzy gave Gwen their thanks for such a nice event, then left the trail near to where they had entered it.

Near the gate, they caught up with Annalise and Merida. Merida was busily engaged in eating her large egg.

"That was fun!" Izzy said. "Did you enjoy it?"

"It was tolerable," said Merida. "Do you think Lent and Easter are just an exercise in delayed gratification?"

"Quite possibly so," said Penny.

"Or perhaps it is deeper than that," said Izzy, who found eleven-year-old Merida's precocious fondness for long words charming, but wasn't going to let her fail to grasp the religious meaning of Easter.

"Monty found a horseshoe."

They showed Annalise and Merida Monty's treasure. "Well done, Monty!" said Annalise. "It's quite a big one, from a working horse, I expect. I hope you will hang it up somewhere for good luck."

"We could do that," said Penny.

"Tips up, mind!" said Annalise.

"Sorry?" Penny said.

"Hang it with the tips facing upwards. If you put it the other way up, the good luck will drain away."

"Will do," promised Penny.

"Monty has brought us the best kind of treasure," said Izzy.

"People who believe in lucky horseshoes are just victims of confirmation bias," said Merida, shoving a shard of chocolate egg in her mouth.

"Well, I declare it to be good luck," said Penny. "What a good boy!" She looked around for Monty and realised he was nowhere in sight. "Monty?"

"You have lost your dog," said Merida unhelpfully.

"Temporarily," said Penny.

"You should meditate on that when declaring horseshoes to be lucky," the girl added.

"Merida!" said Annalise sternly.

Merida shrugged, folded her half-eaten egg away in its golden foil and stood. "We can help you look for him," she said.

Penny turned round, calling. "Monty!"

"Some help might be appreciated," said Izzy. "One might even say we are lucky to have you with us."

Merida humphed, but seemed amused by the notion.

41

The four of them walked back into the copse, going against the gentle flow of egg hunters coming the other way.

"Sorry, sorry," said Penny. "We're just looking for my dog."

From somewhere further ahead there came a sudden and piercing scream. Izzy didn't think screams and missing dogs were intrinsically linked, but there was something about the nature of the shout that drew her. Abruptly, she was running down the track.

A small knot of people were clustered on the path. At the centre of the group sat a small corgi with mud on his paws and his tongue lolling.

"Monty!" said Penny and rushed forward. She came to a sharp halt when she saw what was at his feet. A long knife with a moulded grip handle lay on the ground in front of

Monty. There were flecks of mud on it; but more than that, there was a dark, drying stain along its blade.

"Did he find that?" said Penny.

But the eyes and ears of the small crowd were not on her, but on two people deeper in the ferns and grasses off the track. The chick with the wobbly undercarriage was consoling a pale and shaken woman.

"It's a body," said a man, nearby. "They've found a body."

"Who is it?"

Izzy looked at the knife on the ground. She knew she'd seen it before. It had been in Geoffrey Carnarvon's hand when he'd helped them dig up their first metal detecting find.

"Some old bloke," someone called.

"Geoffrey?" Penny said to Izzy.

"Everyone stay exactly where there are," said the Easter Bunny, stepping forward.

He grasped his head and hauled it off. Underneath was a face that Izzy did indeed recognise.

"Detective Sergeant Chang!" she said in surprised. "What are you doing here?"

The local police detective gave her a testy look. "Even police detectives get days off," he said, then glanced at the two people standing in the undergrowth. "Some days."

He waded through the grasses and brambles to inspect the unseen body on the ground. He turned and pointed a fat bunny glove at Penny. "You said a name, Miss Slipper!"

"I did?"

"You did."

"Geoffrey," she said. "Geoffrey Carnarvon."

"We think this might be his knife," said Izzy.

His face was taut. He now had his bunny hands off and was making a phone call. After a few words he spoke to the group.

"I am going to need to speak to everyone currently present. Miss King, Miss Slipper – I may need to start with you."

42

It was long past dark by the time Izzy got home.

The police had cordoned off the Brick Lane copse and brought the Easter egg hunt to an abrupt end. There were some tears from younger participants, but these rapidly vanished when Gwen simply gave out the remaining chocolate eggs to them. It was disappointing, but perhaps not unsurprising, to discover it was the eggs bit, not the hunting, that children loved most about such events.

As Detective Sergeant Chang promised, everyone present was questioned by the police. Many of the people present were allowed to go home after providing contact details. There would be dozens of potential witnesses to work through. The cheery bunny costume did nothing to mask DS Chang's weary realisation that he had a mountain of work ahead of him.

Crime scene tape was placed around the area and across the gates. A white tent was erected over the body. A mobile incident room was set up on Brick Lane, and eventually Penny and Izzy were taken inside, one at a time, to answer the police's questions.

Izzy, for her part, explained about how she had come to know Geoffrey recently and had recognised his hunting knife. When DS Chang asked for a description, Izzy did her best to avoid simply saying "He looked like Father Christmas, but with a shorter beard". The detective didn't confirm or deny if her description matched the body, but she could plainly see from the ease with which he accepted her description that it was absolutely Geoffrey Carnarvon's body out there.

She had asked him if Geoffrey had been murdered. He replied with another question, asking why she would think that was the case. At that, she didn't know what to say. To go beyond concrete facts would lead DS Chang down the rabbit hole of theories and speculation regarding Sybil Catchpole, crossword clues, and buried treasure (although bunny Chang and rabbit holes would have been entirely appropriate).

Izzy stuck to the concrete facts and hoped she wouldn't be later accused of withholding evidence.

Eventually, after much waiting, she was permitted to leave and walked home. The night was grey and the air turning chilly. She originally planned to go home and present Marcin with a chocolate egg she had saved from the Easter egg hunt, but her mood was now flat and it didn't seem appropriate.

She called out for him, but there was no reply in the dark house.

I have not been honest with you, Marcin had said.

She put the kettle on for a cup of tea she didn't really want.

I hope you will forgive my secrecy and my foolishness, he had said.

She heard footsteps in the yard outside.

Marcin came through the door. "Izzy, you're home." He smiled, but it was a nervous smile; uncertain. "Please come with me."

"I just put the kettle on for a cup of tea."

"We can have tea shortly. I have something I must show you."

"You wanted to tell me something," she said.

"Yes. And show you something."

Izzy followed Marcin into the yard. He held her hand and led her. She realised where they were heading.

"Are we going to the barn?" Izzy asked. She hoped that it didn't sound too much like she was asking whether she would ever be seen again.

"We are going to the barn."

"Is this the thing you need to confess about?"

"Yes. I acted without thinking and—" Marcin took a deep breath and unlocked the padlock on the door.

He thrust the door wide open. Izzy had to take a few moments to work out what she was looking at. One thing that was very obvious was a set of sheep's fleeces, laid out on a table. She approached and ran her hands across them. They had to be the ones she had been watching on-line, and which had been bought by someone else.

"You bought the fleeces," she said.

"Yes."

"For me?"

"Yes."

"Well, that's—" She looked at him. "That's a nice gift. I don't understand."

"Neither did I," he said. "I thought I would buy you a gift, a new toy, to enable you to break the abstinence of Lent with a brand-new project."

"Right?"

"So, I put a bid in on some machinery." He reached over and turned on a light switch, illuminating the rest of the barn.

Huge pieces of machinery lined the walls, but she didn't know what they were. Or did she? She went over to the first object. Something about the shape of its components was familiar.

"Is this a carding machine?" she asked.

"I thought I would buy you a machine for making wool. Like a fool, I thought it would be like a spinning wheel. You know – from the fairy story *Titelitury*."

"Sleeping Beauty?"

"No, the one about the angry little man who spins straw into gold."

"Rumpelstiltskin."

"Yes! I thought—" He waved a hand at the machinery. "It came from a wool mill in Wales which was closing. It was too big. The project was too big. I wanted to buy you something nice and I bought this monster of a machine."

All of the pieces fell into place for Izzy. The secret trip to

Wales, the strange meetings in the barn, the clanking sounds. "Aubrey helped you to get it going?"

"He did. He is a very practical man."

Izzy knew a little bit about preparing wool from fleeces. Carding was one of the most labour-intensive stages: where the fibres were pulled into long strands by passing them repeatedly between barbed panels to drag them into alignment.

"Did you know the oldest carding machines used teasels?" she said. "The seed heads of the plant? They have little hooks in them to help with the carding." Izzy was giddy with the prospect of what this could mean.

"You like this?" he said. He was genuinely worried that she wouldn't.

"Are you kidding me?" she laughed. "This is the best present you could buy. Oh, my goodness, Marcin. This— Why did you hide it from me?"

"I wanted it to be a surprise and I was ashamed. I thought you would think I was an idiot."

"You are an idiot," she said, feeling a big grin stretching across her face. "A wonderful, beautiful idiot for not telling me about this in the first place." She looked around the barn and all the space still left over where she could already picture additional machines and work benches. Project after project.

"You forgive me?" he said.

"I love you," she said.

"Because I buy a big carding machine?"

She shook her head. "Because you put this much

thought, this much time and effort into making me happy." She wrapped her arms around him and placed a massive kiss on his lips. "But no more secrets," she said.

"No more secrets," he agreed.

43

Easter Monday was a bank holiday and Cozy Craft would be shut for the day. This should have been an opportunity for Penny to have a long lie-in. The best lie-ins require preparation, so Penny got up at her usual time to make herself a cup of tea and then returned to bed with tea, leftover Easter egg, her best dog snoozing on the quilt next to her, and Sybil Catchpole's *The Golden Bell*. She had read and re-read through the gloriously illustrated book several times, although she had yet to understand how the preface could claim there were sixteen pictures when there were only fifteen. Properly provisioned and with a mystery to solve, she reckoned she could stay in bed until eleven at the earliest, perhaps even push through to noon.

However, such plans were interrupted by a phone call from a highly excited Izzy. After listening to Izzy's gabbling enthusiasm for a full minute, Penny said, "Stop. You need to slow down. So I got the part about the fleeces, they are yours after all. I was lost after that."

"So Marcin got me a carding machine! It's huge, from a mill in Wales!"

"Right, right. A carding machine?"

"A carding machine!"

"Izzy, pretend I am really stupid please," said Penny. "So I get my fleece off a sheep. What happens next? Is that called carding?"

"No, you can't do carding until it's clean. So you trim away the really cruddy bits and then wash it. I might use a tub, or even get an old washing machine especially. After that comes the carding, which kind of brushes the fibres so that they are all in a straight line."

"Oh I see," said Penny. "Does spinning come after that?"

"Yes it does. I think that's what Marcin thought he was going to buy me when he'd put the bid on the machine. Just a spinning wheel. Did you know what Rumpelstiltskin is called in Polish?"

"Pardon?"

"Titelitury."

"Er, okay."

"You know the story."

"Oh, I know the story," said Penny. "I always felt sorry for Rumpelstiltskin myself."

"Are you sure we're remembering the same story?"

"Sure we are. She uses him to spin straw into gold, but when he wants payment she decides she no longer likes the terms of the deal."

"He wanted to steal her baby, didn't he?"

"I'm not saying it was a good deal. It's just that we're

supposed to sympathise with the person who wants success without paying for it."

"*Anyway. Spinning wheel. That's what he thought he was buying me, but no, he ends up buying fifty percent of what I need to set up my own micro-wool mill. Have you ever heard of anything more thrilling?*" Izzy asked with a squeal.

Penny thought for a moment. "No, I genuinely haven't, it's very, very exciting, Izzy! And now Lent is over—"

"*Exactly! Oh, the projects we will do! The things we will make!*"

"Yes, I can imagine."

"*But that's not the best bit.*"

"Isn't it?"

"*Don't you see?*" said Izzy. "*I've been a fool. Worrying about Marcin. I'd been building up some very silly ideas in my mind.*"

"You? Silly ideas? Gosh, how surprising."

"*Okay, enough with the sarcasm. I was a fool.*"

"You've said that. Doesn't mean it's not true, but you've said that."

"*All those bad and unkind thoughts and he opens the barn doors and it's all flipped on its head. I should have trusted Marcin more.*"

"Quite possibly true."

"*Most of the time people are just what they say they are. I should learn to look past the doubts and the fears.*"

"And the lies..." said Penny, softly.

"*What lies?*" said Izzy, but Penny was not listening. The words had dropped into her head out of nowhere. It took her a moment to place them, then she realised that they were right in front of her.

"Wait a minute, wait a minute," she said. She flipped back through the copy of *The Golden Bell* to the preface at the front. "Here," she said and read, "*To find the fabled golden bell, there is but one thing you should know: The wisest will look past the lies to find the treasure buried below...*"

"*What's that?*" said Izzy. "*Is that the book?*"

Penny blinked. "I might know where the golden bell is buried," she said.

"*What? Really?*"

"Maybe, maybe, because—" She flung the quilt back, burying poor Monty beneath its folds, and jumped out of bed. "I think I might also know—"

"*Know? Know what?*"

Penny raced down two flights of stairs to the shop floor. Where was it? Where was it? She went to the papers on the little shelf below the counter, rifling through until she found the photographs they'd taken of Sybil Catchpole's encoded journals. She read the front page. "*The secrets of my diaries can be read by simple application of the key below.*"

"*What's that?*"

"I think I also know how to read Sybil's diary."

"*You decoded it?*"

"Sort of. Possibly. We need to go to Avalon Cottage."

"*We gave the key back to Gwen.*"

"Then phone her."

"*You've gone all mad and decisive again.*"

"I know, but I really think I'm onto something. Think you can phone Gwen? Monty and I will meet you there. I think I have the answers!"

44

Izzy caught up with Gwen on Brook Lane, on the way to the cottage. Only a few minutes later she found Penny and Monty on the narrow track leading between the trees to Avalon Cottage.

"Thank you for coming out," Izzy said to Gwen. "I'm sure my cousin has a good reason for this."

"Not a problem, not at all," said Gwen, in the exaggerated tone of someone who wanted everyone to know how perfectly fine she was with everything. "I had very little to do this morning anyway. Just teenagers: notoriously hard to get out of bed and engage in family activities. I'd have just been pottering around at home – which is no way to spend a bank holiday."

There was a lightness to the air that morning, a gentle breeze playing among the green leaves and grass, a sense of a world renewed.

"Huh," said Gwen in suspicion. Izzy was about to ask

what the problem was when she saw the car parked outside Avalon Cottage.

"That's Barry's car," said Gwen.

"Not expecting him to be here?" said Penny.

"He can come and go as he pleases," said Gwen politely. She went to the front door and tested the handle. It was unlocked.

Penny and Izzy and Monty followed her through. The house was quiet, undisturbed since their last visit. There was no immediate sign of Barry.

"Now, I think we should do the diary first," said Penny. "Because if I'm right, it will just show Sybil's way of thinking."

The red and gold diary was back in its place on the bureau.

"Now, if I may," said Penny and approached.

"What the hell is going on?" said Gwen suddenly and loudly, and dashed for the kitchen door.

Izzy frowned and looked to Penny, then saw through the back window. Gwen was hurrying out through the garden and down the lawn. Penny and Izzy went to the window to get a better view. At the far end of the garden the gateway between Sybil's and the Atkinsons' gardens was wide open. Horace and Alison Atkinson were standing by the tall ash tree with Barry Catchpole. Barry appeared to have a small chainsaw in his hand.

Gwen started shouting. Izzy couldn't quite make out the words through the glass, but the meaning was clear enough. The Atkinsons and Barry were planning on cutting down the tree without consulting Gwen. Other voices were raised, and more than a couple of arms were flung into the air.

"Should we go out and try to calm things down?" said Izzy.

"Or—" said Penny and crouched beside the bureau.

"What are you doing?"

"I'm going to feel stupid if I'm wrong," said Penny. "The journal said you can access the diaries with the key below."

She felt around under the writing surface of the bureau desk. "Ha!" she declared.

"Ha?" said Izzy.

Penny stood up. In her hand was a big lump of Blu Tack, and firmly embedded in that was a small, old-fashioned key.

"Where was that?" said Izzy.

"Just stuck under the desk," said Penny.

Izzy stared in wonder. "So when the journal said 'the key below'..."

"It just meant a key below. Sometimes keys are just keys. You yourself said that the *Frambeat* team thought the diary was just gibberish. Well, it was. It is. It's like a good crossword clue. It misdirects. Now we need to 'apply' the key below."

Izzy was instantly beside her at the bureau. "Old desks like these often had hidden compartments. There will be a tiny keyhole somewhere."

Side by side, they worked their way over the surface of the bureau, feeling into crevices and poking carved features.

"Here! Here!" said Izzy, running her fingers around a dark knot in the wood.

Penny slipped the key inside. It fitted. It turned! A slim drawer – spring propelled surely – popped out.

"I can't believe Sybil wrote out a whole journal of pretend code just to hide this," said Izzy.

"She had a playful and creative nature for sure," said Penny.

The drawer was little more than an inch thick, and inside its baize-lined surface was a number of slim notebooks and a small pile of documents. Izzy lifted out the books and Penny took the papers.

On each of the pages of the first notebook Izzy opened were hand-drawn outlines of crossword puzzles. Izzy thought she recognised some of them. Every crossword Sybil had made under the name of Socrates was here, recorded neatly.

"A publisher's rejection of her proposal for a new book," said Penny, glancing at the top letter. "Two – three of them. She kept her rejections." She shuffled through and was quiet for a moment. "Letters, hand-written." She flipped them over. "They're from Ivor."

Izzy peered over Penny's arm to have a look.

"They're from prison," said Penny, scanning through. "*Hate it here ... can't cope ... do something about it...* Look: *Instruct Horace to tell the police the truth.*"

"What truth?" said Izzy.

"It doesn't say. *It hasn't worked ... the children need me ... I don't have the strength for this...*" She flipped to the next. "*Not heard from Horace ... how long does it take? The wheels of justice ... I can't cope...*"

There were nearly a dozen of the letters. Penny passed them to Izzy as she skimmed through each.

"When did Ivor die?" said Penny.

"Eighty-two," said Izzy, then looked at the final letter in

Penny's hand. "That must have been written not long before he drank himself to death."

Though the full meaning was not entirely clear, the intense sadness and desperation in those letters was palpable.

"You go digging around in people's pasts—" said Izzy, not sure where the end of that sentence would go.

"The golden bell," said Penny.

"Pardon?"

Penny had a copy of *The Golden Bell* with her. "I worked out where the diary was. Sybil's clues. There's always a complex explanation and a simple one. I think I know where the bell is buried."

"Really?"

Penny nodded and led the way outside, Monty scampering eagerly at her heels.

45

In the spring sunlight Sybil's garden seemed to be blooming even more than before, and the scene would have been one of a pastoral tranquillity – if not for the four people engaged in a heated row at the far end. Gwen and Horace were doing their best to shout over one another. Penny was just glad that Barry had at least put the chainsaw down on the lawn. The addition of a revving motor would not help matters.

"She's gone! But, with every season, the tree causes us more damage!" said Horace furiously.

"It's not your tree! It's not your land!" Gwen retorted.

"Barry is happy to help, and it *is* his land!"

"We've not had a chance to discuss this!" Gwen hissed.

"You never want to discuss anything sensibly," said Barry.

"Um, can we interrupt?" said Penny, approaching cautiously.

"Oh, it's the Care Bear women!" Barry tutted.

"This is a private matter, Penny," said Horace. "And you can see we're busy."

"But I know where the bell is," said Penny. She held up the book as explanation.

"We don't have time for theories," said Barry.

"It's not a theory, I assure you," Penny continued calmly. "We 'decoded' Sybil's journal. Using the same method I think I can tell you all, right now, where the golden bell is."

"This is neither the time nor the place," continued Horace, but Alison put a hand on his arm.

"Maybe we need to step back. Maybe a change of, um, topic, for a minute. This has all become rather heated."

It clearly pained her to speak so rationally. Sharp, hurtful looks were exchanged all around, but now there was at least a moment of quiet.

"You've deciphered all the clues in the pictures then?" sneered Barry. "Under which hill, or gravestone, or Yorkshire monument is it buried?"

"It's here," said Penny simply.

Horace actually turned around on the spot, as though expecting to see the golden treasure suddenly appear before him.

"The pictures Sybil painted were beautiful," said Penny. "Really. She was a gifted artist, and an even more gifted setter of puzzles. She wasn't beyond puns or jokes. The pictures in this book offer one clue and one clue only. At least I think so. I hope so."

"What clue?" said Gwen.

"There are fifteen pictures in this book."

"Yes?"

Penny held the book out to Gwen. "How many does it say there are in the foreword?"

Gwen, still emotional and far from eager, took the book, opened it and read. *"To find the fabled golden bell, there is but one thing you should know: The wisest will look past the lies to find the treasure buried below... This book contains sixteen pictures which tell—"*

"Sixteen pictures," said Penny. "Thank you. There are fifteen pictures and the preface says there are sixteen."

"So?" said Horace.

"It's a lie. Sybil, in her very own words, tells us a lie. And what should we, the wisest, do?"

Gwen glanced at the page. "Look past the lies to find the treasure buried below."

"And it's all lies," said Penny. "Everything in that paragraph is a lie. So what's below it?"

Gwen looked again. "My mum's name."

"What does it actually say?" said Penny.

Gwen huffed. *"S. Catchpole, Avalon Cottage, Suffolk."*

Penny nodded and raised a finger to point past all of them at the tree, and the little metal plague screwed to the trunk.

"Susan Catchpole, nineteen twenty-seven to nineteen seventy-seven. Or S Catchpole, Avalon Cottage, Suffolk."

It was mildly gratifying to see four pairs of eyes bulging with surprise, although that feeling wouldn't last if Penny was proved wrong. She knelt quickly by the base of the ash tree and began pulling at the earth with her bare hands. Izzy, evidently keen to show her faith in Penny, was by her side in an instant and also digging away. A moment later Monty joined in with the enthusiasm of a recently trained Easter egg snuffler.

"But it's supposed to be buried on public land," Horace protested.

"Lies," said Penny, grunting as she dug. "All lies."

They were lifting out fat loamy lumps of earth now, getting rich soil under their fingernails and in their laps, but Penny didn't care. Izzy moved round the tree to dig between the roots.

"Should I get a spade?" offered Gwen, perhaps a little too late.

Monty was yipping joyfully and scrabbling at the earth in a blur of speed. A claw caught in a piece of cloth and, a moment later, it was scraping against a hard surface. Penny gave him a congratulatory ruffle of his collar and gently moved him aside to bring up what he had found.

It was a smooth white container.

"That's ceramic," said Alison.

"Protection maybe," said Izzy.

It was a sealed cylinder, not unlike a medicine capsule, but nearly the size of a rugby ball.

"This can't be it, surely..." breathed Horace in wonder.

Penny looked it over, seeking out a means of opening it. Finding none, she smashed it down, carefully, over the nearest exposed root. It came apart easily, into two ragged halves, and something tumbled out. The lustre of unblemished gold was unmistakeable and mesmerising.

Monty barked in surprise.

Penny lifted the treasure out of the earth.

"The bell," said Gwen.

"It's real," said Barry.

It was, perhaps, smaller than Penny had expected: the photograph on the back of the book had given no idea of scale. But the weight of the object, the shine, the carefully and artfully placed stones... Its beauty was inescapable.

Penny frowned, a thought coming to her for the very first time. "Is this mine now? Does it belong to me?"

"It's what our mother said in her book," said Barry.

"But it is on our land," put in Gwen.

"Legally, an interesting issue," said Horace. "*Res nullius.* Does it belong to anyone?"

Izzy snapped several pictures of Penny holding the bell in her dirty hands. Penny even managed to smile for a couple of them.

"Pictures of Penny and her treasure will be appearing in the local news very soon, I should think," Izzy said brightly. "I'm recording a video of her now. I'm sure she'll be giving an exclusive interview to the *Frambeat Gazette.*"

"Have it. It will be good to be done with it," said Barry dismissively and stalked towards the house.

"What!" called Gwen. "Where are you going?"

"To make a cup of tea," he said. "I think I need one."

"But the bell!" said Gwen. "It's ours! We found it!"

"No we didn't," he called back. "Anyone of us could have found it, but we didn't. Now, who's for a brew?"

Izzy stood close to Penny. "Oh, my."

"I know," said Penny, turning the bell over in her hands. "It's amazing, isn't it?"

"Not that," said Izzy. "I mean, yes, wow. But I think I've just worked out who killed Sybil. And Geoffrey."

Penny looked at Izzy. Izzy nodded solemnly.

46

Penny followed Izzy down the garden to the house. Barry had filled the kettle and it was beginning to warm up. Penny held up the bell.

"Gold doesn't get rusty, does it?"

"Famous for never tarnishing," said Izzy. She looked at Barry. "I'm sorry to hear about Geoffrey."

His face tightened painfully for a moment as he took cups from an overhead cupboard. "Yeah. A terrible business."

"We only met him a couple of times," said Izzy, "but he seemed really nice."

"Bit of a father figure for you," said Izzy.

Barry put a cup down hard. "Yes," he muttered.

"After a lifetime without your own dad."

"Are you trying to make me more miserable?" he said, bitterly.

Alison Atkinson popped her head in through the back door. "Does anyone need any help?"

"Actually, we do," said Izzy. "Penny and I have been trying to solve the mystery of Sybil's death."

"I ... sort of meant with the tea things," said Alison.

"Don't worry, we're nearly there," said Izzy.

"Are we?" said Penny.

"You see, it was all very confusing," said Izzy. "Sybil died last year from foxglove poisoning. It didn't seem like an accident, because Sybil was very knowledgeable about plants." Izzy touched the shelf of clean and empty jars on the wall. "It didn't seem like suicide – despite her possibly wishing to bring her terminal illness to an end – it didn't seem like suicide because she had carelessly left the fatal seeds mixed in with her regular herbal tea, where anyone else might drink it. It seemed to be murder. But then there was the problem of the crossword."

"Oh, that crossword!" Alison tutted. "Pure chance."

"Homicide. Foxglove. Digitalis. Garden. Botanical. Poison. Sybil. An amazing chance if true," said Izzy. "What are the odds?"

"Our doctor friend told us there really wouldn't have been time, once poisoned, for Sybil to fashion a crossword and pop it in the post," said Penny. "And it's a truly odd method of communication."

"We considered it might have been suicide, but she wanted to make it look like murder. That Sybil wanted to frame someone. For that she would really have to hate someone."

"We didn't know who, though," said Penny.

"I think I do now," said Izzy.

"You do?" said Penny surprised.

Izzy nodded. "There was one person who, in the end, Sybil truly came to hate."

"Who?"

Izzy picked up the pile of Sybil's letters from the counter. "We found Sybil's old correspondence. There was the clue in the coded journal."

"Where?" said Barry in disbelief.

Izzy pointed through to the lounge. "A secret compartment in the bureau, and a key stuck to the underside. Very simple really."

"I worked that bit out," said Penny, keen to show she was involved, even though she didn't know where Izzy's explanation was going.

"Perhaps we need to get Horace and Gwen to hear this," said Alison, looking nervously towards the garden.

"Perhaps not," said Izzy. She flicked through the letters. "In these letters which Ivor sent to Sybil from prison, he told her how unhappy he was. I've never been to prison, but I guess it's not a bed of roses. He was depressed, miserable, and he repeatedly asked Sybil to get Horace, as the family solicitor, to tell the police the truth."

"What truth?" said Alison.

"You yourself said that Geoffrey, when he got out of prison, came here and wanted to know about the letters. He wanted to know why Ivor hadn't been released yet."

"It made no sense," said Alison.

"I don't suppose it would. Ivor had gone to prison for a very clear crime. He'd been drinking. That man, Ken

Bickerthwaite, was hit by a car and died. Open and shut case, as they say. You'd all been out drinking that night," said Izzy.

"The pub in Yoxford," said Alison.

"And there was that phrase Horace used."

"Ivor had ... drunk enough whisky to anaesthetise a cow," supplied Penny.

"A buffalo actually," said Izzy. "But yes."

"He was very drunk," said Alison. "We all were."

"I know anaesthetised buffalos aren't an exactly scientific measure, but I do wonder," said Izzy, "if in fact Ivor was far too drunk to drive at all."

"Evidently not," said Alison.

"I mean, he wasn't even driving," said Izzy.

Penny frowned, then her eyebrows went up. "Sybil was driving the car?"

"Alison herself said, in the aftermath – when the news came out – Sybil might as well have mown down that poor chap herself."

"Sybil *was* driving," said Penny. "That makes sense."

"Oh, really?" said Barry snidely.

Penny was starting to see it. "Sybil was driving because her husband, your dad, was too drunk to take the wheel. Then the accident happened. Beyond the mere tragedy of that fact, it was terrible news for the newly famous author, Sybil Catchpole."

"But Ivor told the police it was him."

Penny smiled sadly. "Something Gwen said the other day. Parents: they would do anything for their children. Perhaps Ivor saw that either Barry and Gwen's mum could face prosecution and prison – resulting in the loss of a mother, along with the reputation and money for the phenomenally successful Sybil Catchpole – or, the embarrassing alcoholic Ivor Catchpole could confess and save both the family and their source of income."

"He lied?" said Alison.

Izzy nodded. "Lied to protect his family, and went to prison."

"You don't know any of this," said Barry.

"It fits," said Izzy.

"But then the reality of the situation hit him," said Penny. "Prison was unbearable. He couldn't go through with it. He wrote to Sybil. He wanted her to put the record straight. He almost certainly told his cellmate, Geoffrey."

"Who knows?" said Izzy. "Maybe he would even have contacted Horace directly, or sought fresh legal assistance and made it all public – except then he died. Prison alcohol. Was it deliberate? Was it an accident? I can't see how we'll ever know."

"All that time, Sybil had what she wanted. She got to enjoy her wealth and her children. She strung Ivor along, or maybe just stopped responding to his letters. She let her children think their father was a selfish, unloving drunkard of a man." Penny couldn't help but think of Rumpelstiltskin, horribly betrayed while the selfish princess spun straw into gold.

"And that was when I worked out who Sybil Catchpole hated above all other people," said Izzy.

"Who?" said Alison.

"Herself." Izzy sighed. "You told us she was self-centred and bitter, Alison. She was ambitious. She was driven. And at the end of it all, when she had nothing to show for it, while the disease ate her from the inside, who did she hate? She hated herself."

"But you said that the hating bit was about making her suicide look like murder," said Alison. "To frame someone."

Izzy nodded. "Yes. Strike that; turn it on its head. In truth, she turned her murder into a suicide."

"Oh, come now. This is nonsense," said Alison.

Izzy was undeterred. "Someone did come in here and put foxglove seeds in her tea mix. But she simply could not have drunk it there and then because, well, there's the crossword."

Penny felt she got it. "She saw what had happened. She saw the seeds. She knew what had occurred. Someone was trying to kill her."

"And I think she knew who and why," said Izzy.

"So, she wrote the crossword, posted it, and quite deliberately completed the murder that had been plotted against her."

"That's too incredible," said Alison.

Izzy smiled. "She wrote crosswords under the name Socrates. In the end Socrates killed himself by drinking poison because he had committed the crime of corrupting the young people of Athens. That kind of symmetry would have truly appealed to the puzzle-maker in her nature."

"The crossword. Was it an accusation or a confession then?" said Penny.

"Both?" shrugged Izzy. "Ivor – accident. Sybil – homicide."

"So who do you think killed her?" said Barry.

Penny looked at the kettle which had switched itself off,

and the letters in Izzy's hands. "There would have been no way of knowing who wanted her dead," she said. "None at all – until Geoffrey died."

"What has Geoffrey got to do with this?" said Alison.

"Absolutely everything," said Penny. "You see, only two people in the whole world had known what happened on the night of the car accident: Sybil and Geoffrey. Ivor had told him, in prison."

"Geoffrey killed her," said Barry.

"Possible, but unlikely," said Izzy. "If Geoffrey wanted to carry out revenge on behalf of his dead cellmate, he could have done it twenty years ago, when he first came here."

"Geoffrey knew, but carried the secret," said Penny.

"Why would he do that?" said Alison.

"Barry and Gwen had lost their dad. What justice would be served if they also lost their mum?"

"I don't know what kind of man Geoffrey was in his youth," said Izzy, "clearly a bad one to end up in prison, but the Geoffrey I met seemed a thoughtful and caring individual – and not just because he had that cheery Santa vibe going on."

"But he couldn't keep that secret forever, I guess," said Penny.

"Things burn inside people. I had to give up something important to me for Lent, and to keep things pent up— It's hard."

"He waited maybe nearly twenty years, then it came out. Only recently. And even after Sybil's death he didn't know someone had acted on that information. He didn't know she had been murdered until we happened to mention it at the funeral."

"He definitely took a funny turn when we mentioned it," said Izzy.

"We do have a tendency to open our mouths when we shouldn't," Penny agreed.

"And he might have known sooner if he'd had chance to look at the crossword we tried to show him."

"Except it got screwed up and thrown away before he could see it."

"Very deliberately screwed up and thrown aside," said Izzy.

The two of them were now looking at Barry Catchpole.

47

It took Alison a long moment to realise where their gazes were directed.

"Barry? Not Barry," she said. "Tell them this is stupid, Barry."

Barry said nothing. His hand was gripping the handle of the quiet kettle. There were cups, but no teas poured.

"You told us yourself on Saturday," said Penny. "Something about dads. You said when we think of our dads we have this memory of men who loved us, who always wanted us, would do anything to protect our mums and us. But you – you had been given a memory that was—"

"Hollow and nasty," said Barry.

"Like the memory bears, you said," added Izzy. "Gwen would be happy with fragments of memory twisted into something she could love. But you... Once Geoffrey had told you, you no longer had that. You saw your mum for what she really was. Sybil Catchpole was the woman who had selfishly stolen your own dad from you."

"So you set out to kill her," said Penny.

"So I set out to kill her," said Barry.

"Geoffrey said you knew your plants."

"No," said Alison, horrified.

"Except mum saw through it," said Barry. "She saw what I had put in the tea."

"And then," said Penny, "weird, strange woman who could not resist a puzzle that she was, she wrote her final one – the crossword – then drank the tea you had provided."

"Maybe the final clue she left was the method of her death," said Izzy. "Socrates, punished with poison for crimes against the young."

"Then we, with our big mouths, effectively told Geoffrey what had happened. Just as a simple confession had revealed the truth about your mum to you, so Geoffrey saw in an instant what you had done."

"Did you kill him?" Alison asked Barry.

"He accosted me," he said. "We argued, in the woods. He has a temper when he lets it show." There were tears in his eyes. "I did – I did love him like a dad."

In the silence that followed there was shout from outside.

"Are you going to come and sort out your dog?" demanded Horace testily. "He's digging up the bulbs!"

Penny took a deep breath and looked at Barry's ashen and downcast face.

"Here's the thing," she said. "The police will know soon enough that you killed Geoffrey. I guess there'll be fingerprints on the knife or something."

"Oh, God..." he whispered.

"But your mum, Sybil. Her death was officially an accident."

"You are suggesting he should get away with it?" said Alison with unexpected anger.

"Think of Gwen. For decades Geoffrey carried the secret of what really happened between Sybil and Ivor. Look what the truth did to Barry."

There were tears pouring down the man's cheeks now.

"The truth is rarely kind," said Izzy.

Penny nodded. "I think we'd best get our dog and go."

They went out into the back garden. Penny slipped Monty's lead on, and together they took him back through the house. Barry was on his mobile, already calling the police.

"What's going on?" said Gwen as she entered the kitchen.

"I am making a cup of tea," said Alison, keeping her voice firmly under control.

Penny and Izzy stepped out of Avalon Cottage and pulled the door shut behind them.

PENNY HELD the golden bell loosely in her hands as they walked down the track. "I don't know how I should feel about this."

"Cursed treasure from a tragic family?"

"Well, not quite. It's got to be worth a lot."

"Tens of thousands of pounds, easily."

Penny puffed her cheeks. "What would I do with that kind of money, eh?"

Izzy hummed lightly. "May I suggest that you invest some of it in *King's Wool Mill Incorporated*?"

Penny laughed. "Is that what you're going to call your new wool business?"

"Maybe. Or ... the *Ewe-nique Wool Company*?"

"*Izzy's Woolly Thinking* more like."

"Ha! Well, it's in pleasant surroundings, so maybe *A Loom with a View*."

Penny groaned. "*Knit Wit Wool Ltd*."

Izzy laughed. "Do I sense a critical tone, Penny? Maybe I won't bring you on board as a partner."

It was Penny's turn to laugh. "I'm surprised you would want me as business partner, considering how much I constrain your wildest excesses."

Izzy grabbed her cousin's arm and pulled her close as they walked down the lane.

"Let's face it, I don't know what I'd do without you," she said. "And you know that too."

Penny smiled. Monty barked at passing birds but the birds simply didn't care.

ACKNOWLEDGMENTS

In the late nineteen-seventies, British artist and illustrator, Kit Williams, created a book called *Masquerade*. The fifteen beautiful pictures it contained provided clues to a golden hare he had buried somewhere in England. The book sold hundreds of thousands of copies and inspired a wave of 'armchair detective' treasure hunts. Though the treasure was found in 1982, the book remains a beautiful work and I heartily recommend you read it if you get a chance.

Sybil Catchpole's *The Golden Bell* is a deliberate and fond homage to *Masquerade*. However, it is important to note that Sybil's personality and the events of her life bear no relation at all to Kit Williams or the story of *Masquerade*.

The cryptic crossword clues in this book were devised by friend and editor, Joel Hames, and I'm very grateful for his help and forever stunned by the way his brain works.

ABOUT THE AUTHOR

Millie Ravensworth writes the Cozy Craft series of books. Her love of murder mysteries and passion for dressmaking made her want to write books full of quirky characters and unbelievable murders.

Millie lives in central England where children and pets are something of a distraction from the serious business of writing, although dog walking is always a good time to plot the next book

Printed in Great Britain
by Amazon